I0726301

ABAYA:
A NOVEL

MARGARET DRAKE

WORKBOOK PRESS LLC
187 E Warm Springs Rd,
Suite B285, Las Vegas, NV 89119, USA

Website: https://workbookpress.com/
Hotline: 1-888-818-4856
Email: admin@workbookpress.com

Ordering Information:
Quantity sales. Special discounts are available on quantity purchases by corporations, associations, and others.
For details, contact the publisher at the address above.

Library of Congress Control Number:

ISBN-13:   000-0-000000-00-0 (Paperback Version)
                000-0-000000-00-0 (Digital Version)

REV. DATE: 09/14/2022

Abaya: A Novel

By

Margaret Drake

Previous novels by this author:

(2018) *Men's Receiving Ward*

(2016) *Blackmail behind the Barracks*

(2011) *Haole Wife*

(2009) *Haole Teacher*

(2008) *Homesteading Woman*

(2005) *Sanatorium Girl*

(2004) *The Disappearing Patient. A novel about an occupational therapist*

(2003) *Reconstructing Soldiers: An Occupational Therapist in WWI*

Memoire:

(1983 & 2010) *A US Feminist in Saudi Arabia: 1980-1982.*

Textbooks:

(1992) *Crafts in Therapy and Rehabilitation*

(1997) *Crafts in Therapy and Rehabilitation* edition 2

Website:

http://www.margaretdrake.com

Table of Contents

ᴀPPRECIATIONS

My Birmingham, Alabama friend, Mary Jane Haden, wanted to write the fictionalized version of my time in Saudi Arabia in the late 80s. But she died of cancer before she could do it. However, she put the idea in my head three decades ago.

Because the main characters are nurses, I want to give credit to nurses I have known and worked with. Nurses have taught me so much about caring, about the healthcare systems, and about friendship. Special relationships with nurses I have known started with my sister Jean Bruning, who did every kind of nursing, ending her career as a school nurse, then other school nurses at elementary schools where I taught, then Jackie Tiller and Mary Hipp with whom I taught in the University of Riyadh, and the many nurses with whom I worked in Los Angles County Acton Alcoholic Rehabilitation Center, Dominguez Valley Hospital, City of Hope, Lynwood Care Center and University of California Irvine Medical Center, Selma Medical Center in Alabama, Louisville Hospital in Mississippi, Kau Hospital on Hawaii Island, as well as my licensed practitioner nurse, nephew Roger Goodell. The nurses, who took my graduate classes at the University of Alabama at Birmingham, and at the University of Mississippi Medical Center, also taught me as much as I taught them. Nurse Peggy Heisman and nephew Roger Goodell, both nurses, edited the last draft of this manuscript.

My nephew Dwane Goodell is the car-guy who was able

to tell me what cars were popular in Saudi in 1980. I was too busy noticing other things to notice which car models were on Riyadh streets. Another nephew, Martin Wagner (Marty) was my lifestyle consultant. Emmet Judziewicz, a botanist friend, advised on tansy. Dr. Michelle Mitchell confirmed some of my musings about spontaneous abortions. And my Saudi students and colleagues unwittingly educated me about the Saudi culture. Michael Atallah, an old friend from Saudi days provided specific details of the Riyadh International Christian Fellowship.

Mary Strong, computer whizz, helped when the computer decided to do its own formatting rather than mine.

Preface

Set in the same era in which the author worked in Saudi Arabia, the main character Elizabeth Adams is not the author though she may have fictionally experienced many similar situations and events. The author's experiences in the Kingdom of Saudi Arabia during the early 1980s provide the background for this story, though all characters in this novel are fictional.

Arabic names and words in this story have been transliterated according to the Library of Congress system. Arabic words are italicized. A glossary of Arabic words in this novel is on page 199. Most Arabic terms are explained at first use.

The reference list on page 201 includes several books from that era, the last half of the twentieth century in that geographic region and about Islam.

Page 202 has a map of the region with the main countries and cities mention in this novel.

The cast of characters in this novel are listed on page 203 in the order in which they appear in the novel. With so many Arabic words and names, this list is to assist the reader to easily keep track.

Chapter 1

Athens Conference Hotel

Fall 1983

Elizabeth stood beside the curtain on the side of the stage at the conference listening to the moderator of this section describe her in terms she hardly recognized. She could see the late conferees entering and exiting the hotel conference room. Ten minutes were allocated between sessions for attendees to move between hotel meeting rooms. As she listened to the moderator giving a glowing description of her career, her mind slipped back to her unsophisticated rural California childhood and the women who had inspired her to reach beyond her humble beginnings. There was her Aunt Phyllis who had been her home economics teacher, her music teacher and her science teacher, also. This woman had raised her family and then helped the community by teaching when others were unavailable in the shrinking population of those willing to teach in rural schools. Then there was her other Aunt Sephrena who taught Sunday school, led the 4-H Club and was on the board of the County Republican Party. Another influential teacher had been Mrs. Planchette, the late middle aged wife of the county attorney who graced the rural high school with her inspiring and sophisticated teaching of communication skills. Mrs. Planchette had given Elizabeth the confidence she needed to step out before an audience and speak clearly. The memory of these women calmed her as she proceeded out to the podium to speak on her years of nursing in Saudi Arabia. To bolster her confidence, she decided that she was really speaking to them, to Aunt Phyllis, Aunt Sephrena and Mrs. Planchette, rather than to a room full of professional nurses.

She knew that she looked spectacular in the embroidered blue silk *galabaya*, a caftan. She had purchased it in the new Women's Souq in the Riyadh mall. Elizabeth felt well prepared to deliver her case study of the nursing program at National Saudia University for Girls. The conference organizers had sought her out to be one of the keynote speakers for this opening session for 'Educating for Cross-cultural Nursing.' Three years ago, when she left her job in a Los Angeles community hospital to teach in Riyadh, she would never have anticipated being invited as a keynote speaker to this prestigious nursing conference in Athens. Her career had been modest before the Saudi Arabian adventure. She had graduated first from a community college associates nursing program and then gone on to the state college to get her bachelors. One of her faculty members at the state college encouraged her to go on to the Masters of Nursing program. She had done that while working the 11 PM -7 AM shift in the medical-surgical ward of the community hospital. This allowed her to do some of her studying in the quiet early mornings before the patients awoke to be prepared for surgery. She had supervised student nurses from the local community college during one summer session when she worked the day shift as she had no classes but was working on her thesis. She took the topic of supervising student nurses on the medical-surgical ward as her thesis topic. This required her to use the libraries of the hospital and the university to learn what had already been written on her topic. She felt she had become quite an expert on nursing education during that effort. Additionally, she had interviewed old retired nursing faculty to see how things had changed. Her thesis was good enough that one of her own faculty members had helped her revise and digest it for submission to a nursing journal. After she finished the master's degree, she was recruited to teach a class in her former community college nursing program.

The room was full when she took the podium. The people in the room wore colorful clothing of all cultures and different styles. Though U. S. nurses no longer wore the ubiquitous white uniforms and winged caps, they usually had some uniform and at events such as this, they did enjoy wearing street clothes as they tired of wearing whatever uniforms their institutions required. Conferences offered an opportunity to dress up and wear dangling earrings which were forbidden for nurses to wear almost everywhere in all hospitals. Many women wore the formal costume of their own country. There were a few male heads scattered about the room, and most of the men too took this opportunity to dress up, too. The men in the room all seemed to be Westerners. Elizabeth did not see any turbans or *gutrahs* in the crowd. There were a few women wearing headscarves but none with covered faces. There were no Saudis in the crowd, she concluded. Her paranoia about having someone report on her presentation back to the Dean the School of Health Sciences of National Saudia Women's University abated. She could be more frank with this assurance.

The recession going on at home in the USA meant that wages were stagnant for nurses as well as for everyone else. Elizabeth realized that it might be the reason this room was so full to hear her. Saudi Arabia had begun to strongly recruit western nurses, for hospital work as well as to teach in the new nursing schools. Salaries offered were way beyond what they could earn at home. The Dean of the School of Health Sciences of National Saudia Women's University had hinted when she approached him about traveling to this conference, that her success in attracting Western nurses to work in Saudi Arabia might result in substantial other benefits. 'Western' in this context usually meant professionals from the United Kingdom, Australia and Canada as well as the USA.

For one brief moment she thought of her old boyfriend Graham Brown, a high school math teacher, who awaited her back in the hotel. The two of them had agreed to meet here in an Athens hotel for a little tryst. When she had agreed to take the job in Saudi Arabia, Graham had been furious with her. They had been lovers for over a year having met at a church singles party. He had assumed that their causal love life was settled. Elizabeth, on the other hand, since their love life had not progressed into anything deeper, was focused on her nursing career. The chance to make a lot more money than she could make in the USA hospitals while teaching young women, as compared to standing on her feet in a maternity ward or surgery theater for eight hours per day, was too good an opportunity to pass up. Shoving this thought back out of her consciousness, she stepped to the podium.

She opened with an introduction which matched the first slide in the carrousel that she had given to the conference audio-visual coordinator. It showed the front of the new marble covered National Saudia University for Girls Administration Building. It looked like the palaces of many of the princes in the new section which had been built near the new embassy buildings. The Administration Building was very grand but because of the Saudi aversions to showing the human body, no students or teachers were included in the picture. Rather, it featured the huge potted palms leading to the huge brass-framed glass double doors and the small brick bordered flowerbed with a fountain. She had gotten this slide from the public relations officer as it had been taken from the top of the 14 foot wall which surrounded the University compound. The compound walls were not visible in the slide. Consequently, it did not illustrate the claustrophobic feeling Western women sometimes got from being confined inside these high-walled compounds.

Elizabeth explained first how she had always been interested in adventure and in other cultures. Los Angeles area was rich in diverse cultures. She told the audience of her encounter with a male National Saudia Girls University administrator, the Dean of the School of Health Sciences, at this same Cross-Cultural nursing conference four years ago in Miami and how he had described the plan for their new nursing program. He had seen her name on the article in the nursing education journal. He began to recruit her that day. The woman Jessie Edwards, whom he had already hired as director of the nursing program was also at the conference. He introduced the two women. They hit it off well. Between the two of them, Jessie Edwards and the administrator, they convinced Elizabeth to leave her job in Los Angeles and come teach medical surgical nursing skills to women students in Riyadh, Saudi Arabia. She did not realize at this time, that all deans in universities were men, as women could not be put in positions over men. His office was near, but just off the women's campus.

Next she showed a slide of the building where female faculty lived next to the University Hospital. She followed this with a photo which she had surreptitiously taken of the little man at the front door called 'The Watch Dog' by the female residents. His job was to make sure there was no mixing of the sexes. Elizabeth had a tiny camera with which she had taken the various photos surreptitiously. Had one of the *mutawahs*, the religious police, seen her, he would have confiscated the camera and perhaps struck her with his stave. Elizabeth was reticent in telling this crowd about her own flouting of this rule as well as the ones forbidding consorting with men. There were so many western men alone in Riyadh that her position as a single Western female made her a sought-after companion and confident. She had many opportunities to break the rules because as a foreign professional, though she was supposed to, she did not require a man to accompany her everywhere like Saudi women did. She liked male companionship. But it did not fit the persona she was trying to present as a role model for Saudi women nursing students so those adventures were not part of this story. She was walking the fine line between trying to inspire other nurses to want to teach in Saudi Arabia and to give a flavor of what life there was really like, and the opportunities for adventure.

Her third slide was of the girls in the class who had insisted that they cover their faces for the photo, as their families might punish them if they discovered they had allowed themselves to be viewed by men at this conference. It also gave a bit of the flavor of what it felt like to be unable to see the faces of the women, the people, with whom you are dealing. Whenever she took the students to grand rounds or clinics where there were male doctors or attendants, the girls always covered their faces. It was a dilemma she dealt with daily, about how to provide the most effective nursing with the handicap of having your face covered.

In the next slide, she showed one of her Egyptian colleagues who had modeled the partial face-cover used by some female doctors when dealing with male patients. The face veil was pulled across one eye leaving the other eye on view. As she looked out over the audience, in the end of the third row from the front where they was enough light from the dim wall sconce on the side aisle, Elizabeth recognized the face of her former colleague who had left she and another member of the National Saudia University for Girls faculty in the lurch. Hadn't she been drummed out of the profession by the California Board of Registered Nursing? This nurse Patsy Elgin, who had taught infectious disease nursing in National Saudia University for Girls, had wanted to travel to tour Pakistan during the Hajj break. The University required her to pay a two month security deposit in order to return her passport to her for the trip. Or she could get two of her nursing faculty colleagues to sign a paper promising to pay the two months salary should she fail to return. This was their way of preventing a faculty member from fleeing before their contract was over. Elizabeth was one of the faulty who agreed to sign that they would pay her bond. Patsy never returned and Elizabeth and Aisha had to pay a month salary apiece before they could regain their own passports and take their summer home leave. As she recalled this, she wondered at the audacity of this woman to show up at her presentation. She wondered if Patsy was still a member of the Nurses' Association. Elizabeth and

Aisha had considered reporting her to the Association, but the requirements of their teaching load had caused them to postpone and postpone until they forgot. But someone else had reported her. It was pretty nervy for Patsy to show up here. She probably thought she could attend unobserved. But apparently the only seat left when she came in was near the light sconce. Well, Elizabeth couldn't think about that now with a room of over one hundred people waiting for her next 'wisdom.'

The fifth slide was of the teenage third wife of a government official holding her new baby boy. The baby was beautifully visible but the mother's face was completely covered, no eyes, nothing but a black shape. The viewer could not tell whether she was looking at the baby or at the camera. Elizabeth described how the husband, the Saudi government official was also the father of one of her students by his first wife, who was an uneducated Bedouin woman whom he had married when she was only 15. Now she was forty and the mother of two girls older than this third wife. She went on to explain that it was necessary to put aside judgment when helping mothers delivery babies, when helping families of whatever form, have the best birth experience. If any in her audience was seriously considering taking a job in Saudi Arabia, they needed to consider whether they could accept such situations without judging.

She showed slides of the Filipina nurses and Korean nurses. One of the Filipina nurses had helped her get secretly into the nursing hostel compound to photograph their living conditions compared to the ones provided for American and British nurses. Their rules were much stricter and privileges much diminished. While American nurses might be required to share a flat, they always had their own bedroom. The Filipinas had to share bedrooms. A Western woman had to be over fifty years old or have a doctorate, before the University would allow her to have a private flat to herself. Elizabeth discovered that their rationale was that women under fifty of any nationality might still be able to attract and entice male visitors. The officials assumed that a flat-mate would discourage such unlawful behavior.

During the Question and Answer period at the end of her presentation, she was surprised at some of the naïve questions she got. Did her patients speak English? Were men allowed into the delivery room? Were antiseptic procedures followed? And then there were questions she had decided not to approach in her presentation about infibulations and clitorectomies. Fortunately, the moderator put off her last questioner before she was about to describe a situation with a young mother who delivered twins through an infibulated vagina. Elizabeth received a vigorous round of applause. Patsy Elgin had slipped away out the side door before the overhead lights came on. The room had to be cleared for the next speaker. Several of the audience followed her from the meeting room and she agreed to meet with them in the coffee shop in the hotel to carry on further conversation about what could be expected if they took a job in Saudi Arabia. First she must pick-up her slide carrousel from the audio visual coordinator. She would also call the other hotel and leave a message for Graham that she couldn't make lunch but they could get together for dinner.

Chapter 2

Flight 601 to the Middle East

After the Dean recruited her to join the nursing faculty and to develop the new curriculum, she waited to hear from him. Saudi Arabia did not offer short term visas except for the pilgrimage. She had to get an *igama* 'workers' visa. But the Dean was eager enough to get her into the country that he made it happen quickly.She had received a confirmation of her contract offer to teach at National Saudia University for Girls over the phone from the clerk in the consulate employment office in Houston. This man who had almost no accent explained that she would need to fill out the papers he was sending and return them as soon as possible. The envelope would contain a work visa application, an employment application and contract, as well as instructions for how to proceed once they sent her tickets for her flight which she should receive as soon as her paperwork was processed. He said the address of the Saudi Consulate in Los Angles would be included. After she has completed this paperwork, she should take it to the Saudi consulate and they would telefax it to Houston so they could complete the contract before sending the tickets. They offered a third more salary than she was making between her hospital job and the community college job combined.

There additionally was a booklet from the University with the following advice:

> For women: In the city street, foreign women are most confortable in long skirts and long sleeves with conservative colors. Sleeveless dress, low cut necklines, shorts or miniskirts are not tolerated since Moslem law requires women to be dressed in modesty. Around the house, shirtwaist dresses, blouses, skirts and pants with tunics can be worn. You may want to bring along with you some long dresses for evening wear. And if you sew, you will want to bring your sewing machine.

Elizabeth took them at their word and shipped her sewing machine as well as her musical instrument and typewriter.

There was time for one more 'women's group' meeting before she would leave. This group of friends had been meeting for the past two years once a week to read and respond to feminist literature. There was a school psychologist, a property manager, a teacher, a hospital employment office administrator, a county government statistician and a housewife in the group. They met in each other's homes. The previous week, when they met in her small compact California bungalow, she had told the women that she was thinking of taking the job in Saudi Arabia. Those feminists were horrified at first but eventually were able to enjoy her excitement in anticipating such an adventure. However, they continued to express their dismay about what might happen to her in the tense Middle East. The county statistician seemed to know way more than Elizabeth did about the situation in the Middle East. Elizabeth thought perhaps it was because she was Jewish and paid more attention to what happened there because of Israel. Anyway, she thought she would be able to spend one more evening with them at least before she departed.

Also, there would be one more opportunity to attend a meeting of the area Medical Surgical Nurses' Association. Though she knew she would miss the camaraderie she experienced with her professional colleagues, she was less fearful of missing them. She had grown much closer to the women in the 'women's group.' She knew she would miss them more.Also, she suspected they were better letter writers. In the 'women's group,' they discussed their love lives, their careers, their aspirations and their family obligations. Though Elizabeth had no intimate family now that she was divorced, she had siblings. One sister lived nearby in Pasadena. Her sisters kept regular contact through a 'round robin' letter.

And then there was her anxiety about telling Graham Brown she would be leaving him for overseas adventure.

She knew she would miss her cozy little bungalow. She had finally saved a down-payment a year ago after finishing her master's degree. Buying this little house felt like a triumph after years of feeling cramped into studios and one bedroom apartments. Even before her divorce, when she and her technician husband could afford more room, she had felt cramped. Perhaps that was because as his drinking got worse, before the final break, there never felt like enough room for them both in the same space.

She had had so little experience with Arabs that she did

not know what to expect. When the movie "Dr. Zhivago" with Omar Sharif came out in 1965, she had been smitten by his sloe eyes. Then there was the Iranian she had met in the doctor's office. She realized that Iranians and Arabs were different but not how much and how both groups disliked being mistaken for the other.

Chapter 3:
Late Summer 1980
Riyadh

Arrival

Within a month of the Miami conference, she rented her house with a fenced back yard to a couple with a dog and was on a plane first to Atlanta, to Rome, then to Jeddah, and finally to Riyadh.

Elizabeth had been remarkably unaware of the recent happenings in the Middle East; the taking over of the Tehran embassy November 5th, 1979, the destruction of the Islamabad USA Embassy November 21, 1979, and the attack on the Grand Mosque in Mecca during the pilgrimage November 21, 1979. Juhayman al-Utaybi and his gang took over the Grand Mosque.

Also, she was unaware of the reforms that the recently assassinated Saudi King Faisal had made such as allowing

Saudi women to avoid covering their faces if they so chose. Those reforms were being reversed due to fears of loss of power by the Royal Family after the Grand Mosque take-over and the revolts in other Middle Eastern countries.

While she had paid attention to the US presidential race between Jimmy Carter and Ronald Reagan, she had not absorbed as so important the Tehran USA Embassy takeover. It was just an event on the other side of the world. In considering working overseas, it was adventure, not danger that was on her radar. So the job offer in Saudi Arabia felt like just an exciting adventure, not a foray into danger.

She had acquainted herself as quickly and as much as possible with the books available in the public library; *At the Drop of a Veil* and a book on the Middle East from the USA State Department. She just figured that she had always been a 'quick study' and would learn as she went along. The Dean who interviewed her in Houston had promised that Arabic language lessons would be available.

She learned something of the Saudi bureaucracy by the requirement to provide notarized letters from previous employers verifying employment dates, a letter from the Secretary of State of California that these notaries were indeed valid and also official transcripts from all higher education institutions. These were sent to the consulate in Houston. Additionally, she had to carry her original diplomas with her to present upon arrival at the university employment office.

In the Atlanta Hartsfield Airport as well as in Rome, Italy, everyone, including Arabic looking people of both sexes, were dressed in the same kind of Western travel clothing as Elizabeth. The only unusual incident was that some airport security personnel came into the final boarding lounge in Rome and began to question a group of Arabic looking men. Since Elizabeth's Arabic language was essentially non-existent at this time, she did not completely understand what they were saying. Eventually, the security personnel left and boarding began. The women were boarded first in what usually was the business class section of the Saudia Airlines flight and the men were directed toward coach. Midway through the flight, the women took turns going to the restroom and returning covered in the black cloak but with the face veil thrown back over the top of their heads. Elizabeth realized then that she was the only woman in the women's section who was not wearing an *abaya*, the cloak she had learned about in *At the Drop of a Veil*. When they disembarked in Jeddah, all women's faces were covered with thick black gauze and bodies were enveloped in the black *abayas*.

Entering the actual Jeddah Airport women's restroom between flights as a number of passengers disembarked here, she was first confronted with an unexpected sight. Hoping to avoid having to use another in-flight restroom, Elizabeth entered and viewed for the first time, a line of black covered women seated along the entire twenty foot wall in the women's restroom anteroom. It was the first of many such experiences, of a line of faceless women staring at her through black face clothes.

As she exited the restroom, she saw in a section near the other side of the lobby, her first mosque with rows of men bowing and prostrating themselves. She would soon learn to recognize the final prayer time of the day. But at this first view she felt puzzled, intrigued might be a better description of her attitude toward this scene. The announcement of boarding for the Riyadh flight waited until prayer-time ended and the group of men arose from the beautifully carpeted airport mosque floor and dispersed. The remainder of the lobby and ticketing area was not carpeted. Clusters of black clad women sat with hand-luggage on the uncarpeted floor around the supporting columns. Their faces were fully veiled as few Saudi women wore the *niqab*, the veil with the slits for eyes.

When Elizabeth's airplane landed at Riyadh International Airport, she saw the carcass of a burned airplane on the parallel landing strip. As she exited the airplane, she asked the stewardess whose English was quite good, what happened to that plane. The stewardess was reticent but just replied "It burned on take-off." It was only later that Elizabeth heard that the cause of this disaster was still being investigated by Saudi Security. Eventually, it was discovered that a Bedouin woman on her way to the pilgrimage, *hajj*, had been cooking over a small butane stove in the aisle. It had tipped and ignited the airplane. Three hundred passengers died, unable to exit the burning airplane. But dying during the *hajj* sent them straight to heaven.

In the waiting area she saw rows of Asian men with leg chains. This gave her pause. But she knew everything was so strange for her at this point that she pushed it from her mind. She was nervous enough about her own wellbeing here that she felt she could not add another anxiety now.

As she approached customs, she could feel people staring at her. Obviously a Western woman with out an *abaya* was very unusual. Suddenly from nowhere, together, appeared four small white robed men. One carried a card with her name on it in English. He shoved it in front of her and pointed to her. Elizabeth nodded her head "Yes." One of the small men took her suitcase out of her hand and another one took her passport from her other hand where she had held it, prepared to show it to the official. They went to the front of the line and she was immediately passed through. None of the people in line grumbled at this taking of privilege which surprised her though things moved so quickly that she hardly had time to examine her surroundings in the airport. Before she knew it, she was deposited in the back of a white Pontiac sedan and two small men were in front. The other two got into another Pontiac also with a government logo on it and followed. They had not returned her passport.

She did her best to examine the night landscape as they went down the seeming main street of the city. However, the lights showed only the palms lining the thoroughfare. The starlit sky was brilliant through the car window. Looking as her wristwatch, Elizabeth realized in was nearly midnight.

Chapter 9

Roommates & Colleagues

The Pontiac sedan and the other following, pulled up to a high stone curb in front of a compound inside high walls with an eight story building and another two story building inside. The wrought iron gate set into the walls was open revealing the ramp to the emergency room marked in English and Arabic on the two story building. While the small man who had been in the passenger seat ran around to the trunk and lifted out Elizabeth's luggage, the driver indicated to her to follow him toward steps leading up into the eight story building of flats. Despite the hour, the blast of desert heat met her as she stepped out of the back seat. At this hour, the wide marble paved lobby was empty but well lit. The driver knocked on the door of a small room which had been built inside the lobby near the front door. A sleepy small man, whom Elizabeth would learn later was nicknamed by Westerners as 'the watchdog,' stuck his head out and realizing who was knocking, handed the driver a key, glanced at Elizabeth and waved them all away. The driver pointed toward the elevator, ushered Elizabeth and her luggage inside and pushed #4.

He tugged her luggage out of the elevator and across the hallway on the fourth floor to the door directly across from the elevator Flat 404. He gestured to Elizabeth to knock. Following his gestured instructions, she waited and heard footsteps inside. The door opened and sleepy-looking blond-haired, short statured woman blinked up at her. The little man behind Elizabeth with the luggage spoke to the sleepy-eyed woman in Arabic. She opened the door more widely and motioned them inside. Inside there was a hallway with doors on either side, and another one at the end. The short woman opened the first door on the left inside the front door and gestured inside. Then she turned to Elizabeth and said, "What's your name? I'm Ina Brook." Elizabeth realized she had a New York accent.

Elizabeth introduced herself and whispered to Ina, "Should I give him a tip?" Elizabeth did not want to start out on the wrong foot here.

"No, Mr. Rahman is a university employee. Picking you up and bringing you here is part of his job," said Ina. "He works for the Dean. We weren't sure when you would arrive so he's been meeting the plane every night for the last few days."

"He still has my passport," Elizabeth said anxiously.

"Oh, they keep all our passports. You won't see that again till you leave. They want to be sure we don't sneak off," said Ina in a voice that sounded pretty sarcastic to Elizabeth who decided it was best to just let it go for the time being.

As Ina was explaining, Elizabeth looked around and realized that the fairly spacious room had not a speck of furniture. There was one tiny window high up on the wall facing the inner hallway. She would have to stand on something to see out that one. Since there was no furniture, she wondered if she was expected to sleep on the floor. Ina said something to Mr. Rahman in Arabic and he put the luggage over against the wall under the tiny window and said, "*Ma Salama*" as he exited the front door.

"What did he say," questioned Elizabeth.

"He was just saying good-bye. Let me show you where your bathroom is. Do you need anything to eat or drink?" asked Ina. She went on, "Do you want to tour our flat tonight or wait until tomorrow? At least let me show you the kitchen tonight in case you need anything. By the way, don't drink the water out of the faucet. It's not pure. I have some pure water in a bottle in the refrigerator." Ina's manner was friendly but business-like, as you would expect of another nurse. She was not offering friendship, simply the best way to get along together.

It was only months later that Elizabeth realized that in the room-arrangement of this flat, her bedroom near the front door with the toilet and shower directly across the hall was intended as the 'men's reception hall' as per Saudi family requirements. Elizabeth's roommate's bedroom and toilet were as far from the front door as possible and would have been used by Saudis as 'the women's section.' This made her able to be much more private. It was only years later that Elizabeth realized how Ina exploited this privacy. In fact, the next day when she toured Elizabeth through the flat, Ina showed her the two common rooms, the kitchen, and the dining room; she did not open the door to her bedroom and the contiguous private bathroom.

Ina explained, "You'll get a furniture increment on your salary to buy whatever furniture you want. But for tonight, I'll lend you a foam mattress and sheets to sleep on." With that she disappeared toward the back of the flat reappearing a few moments later, dragging a colorful canvas covered foam mattress and sheets over her arm.

While Ina was gone, Elizabeth pondered whether or not she had misunderstood the Dean in Houston about the housing allowance. She certainly had been unaware that housing only meant the walls and roof, not the furnishings.

After twenty-seven hours since she left Los Angeles Airport, sleeping on the foam mattress was no impediment to a good nights sleep. She awoke when her roommate stuck her head in the door to say, "I'm off to the office. Jessie Edwards, the boss, I think you met her, yes? She says no need for you to come in today. You can just sleep in. It's a week till classes start so you have plenty of time to get ready."

Elizabeth lifted her head off the bundle of her own clothes that she had fashioned into a pillow and nodded saying, "OK, is there a telephone here in the flat?"

"Yes, I left the office number written on the paper beside the phone. It's in the dining room. I'll be home about two for rest-time. We can talk more then. By the way, Jessie lives right above us on the fifth floor."

Elizabeth awoke several times during the day to use the toilet and drink from the water vessel in the refrigerator. Ina had left a bowl of fruit on the counter with a note saying "This fruit has been washed. It is OK to eat." A banana and apple had kept Elizabeth's hunger pangs at bay. She became aware of the coolness of the flat. It was difficult to realize she was in the desert because there were no windows. The barren room with a thick felt covering on the floor did not stimulate her senses so she immediately drifted off as soon as she stretched out on the foam mattress again. Elizabeth appreciated the coolness as she slept dreamless between visits to the kitchen and toilet. Her knowledge of jetlag symptoms reassured her of the correctness of catching up on her sleep.

Late in the afternoon, she was awakened by a knock on the door and she called out "Just a minute," hoping it was an English speaker who knocked as she knew no Arabic yet. She had slept in her slacks and t-shirt so did not need to cover herself up before answering the door. She immediately recognized Jessie Edwards, director of the nursing school program, from having met her at the Miami conference.

Jessie was a mature woman probably approaching sixty years of age, Elizabeth guessed. She was about five and a half feet tall, a little thickened around the waist but definitely not fat. She wore a long-sleeved embroidered white blouse and floor length dark gabardine skirt. Her hair was curled around her head and face, possibly from a hair-dresser's permanent. She looked kind, benevolent, even.

"Welcome, welcome." She said stepping into the hallway. "We've been waiting for you. I know there's not much furniture here in your room.Would you like to come up to our flat right above you and have some tea?"

"I would like that but I feel like I should take a shower or bath before I get close to anybody. The last shower I had was in Los Angeles and I've been sleeping in these clothes. Can you wait while I do that?" asked Elizabeth.

"Of course, I'll just go back upstairs and come back for you in about half an hour, OK? Ina should be home soon, too, and I know she would not feel comfortable having me waiting back in the dining room," replied Jessie.

Elizabeth ponder the strangeness of Jessie's statement as she ushered her out the door, but she did not feel well enough acquainted with the situation here yet to question her about it. Elizabeth had been raised with sisters who came and went from each others' rooms, borrowed each other's clothes. She was used to feeling welcome almost anywhere. Because she had never lived in a dormitory during college, she had never experienced the territoriality that occurred in congregate living with strangers. It was only much later that she learned that Ina had been the first nurse ever hired by the University. When Jessie came, she usurped Ina's place which Ina resented though Ina certainly had no qualification for running a nursing education program as she was only an LPN while Jessie held a Master of Nursing from the University of Georgia.

As promised, Jessie appeared at the door on time, like a good nurse, and ushered the freshly showered and clean-feeling Elizabeth to the elevator and to her flat. The layout of the flat was exactly like the one directly below it, however, the felt floors were covered with Middle Eastern carpets and the walls had a variety of paintings and framed Arabic lettering. Jessie led Elizabeth back to the dining room area where a brass teapot sat steaming on a tray with tiny cups. Another woman of similar age as Jessie sat at one side of the table.

"This is another of the faculty, Amy Burch. We share this flat. Amy teaches the psychiatry." Jessie indicated a chair for Elizabeth.

Elizabeth registered the Southern accents of both women. She wondered about them since their accents sounded so similar but the two differed greatly in appearance. Amy was several inches shorter than Jessie and slender as a waif.

Her skin was much more wrinkled so she looked older. But her hair was the same steel-gray curly helmet. Both women had blue eyes. Amy wore glasses, was in slacks and was smoking a cigarette. The brass camel shaped ashtray lay at her elbow along with another teacup. Amy poured some tea for Elizabeth and sat the tiny cup in front of her. The tea smelled wonderful though the tiny cup held hardly a mouthful.

"Have you been able to get settled in yet?" Amy asked as she extinguished her cigarette.

"Well, not yet. I was able to find my clean clothes in my luggage. It seems so long ago that I packed those suitcases that I almost forgot where I put everything. But I feel more rested." Elizabeth already felt more relaxed with these two women. She had worked with a variety of charge nurses and had learned how to interact with their various personalities so she was quickly able to assess the comfortable down-home ways of these two new colleagues.

"Saturday, which is their Monday, we'll stop and pick you up on our way to the bus to show you the way to the University. One of the first things you will need to do," explained Jessie, "is to have your health exam in the clinic at the hospital next door. But we can do that Saturday after rest time. The women's clinic reopens after rest time."

Elizabeth listened as the two women explained the university schedule. They tried to get to the university by 8 AM though the Saudi students and Egyptian office workers did not arrive until 9 AM. All nursing classes were held in the morning. At one o'clock in the afternoon, all the female students and faculty went home for rest time. The students were done for the day at one o'clock unless they were scheduled to visit a clinic or hospital. All regularly scheduled classes were within those four hours. This made for tight class scheduling. But with only five students enrolled so far in the nursing program, they discussed the confidence they had that the six faculty members could easily teach the nursing curriculum in that amount of time. The students had studied English but their proficiency left something to be desired.

Jessie went on to tell of how she discovered that the Egyptian nursing faculty were falling back to lecturing in Arabic though the curriculum specified that all teaching was to be done in English. It was a compromise Jessie felt she had to make to allow the students to become competent. She had advised the Egyptian faculty about it as the students would be required to take the nursing exam in English before they could become licensed. This explanation relieved Elizabeth of some of her anxiety about her ignorance of Arabic language.

As they sat drinking their tea, they heard the Muslim call to prayer. It was very close. Jessie led her to the tiny balcony from her bedroom where Elizabeth looked down upon the hospital mosque right below. There were hundreds of pairs of sandals and a few shoes fanning out from the door.

"Tomorrow is Thursday, which is like Saturday at home since Friday is the Muslim Sabbath. We'll take you to the *souq* tomorrow if you like so you can begin to see the city," said Jessie.

Elizabeth readily agreed to this proposal. She was eager to become acquainted with her new surrounding and knew she would need guidance as she couldn't even read the street signs.

She remembered that Mr. Rahman still had her passport so she decided to verify what Ina had said. "Mr. Rahman kept my passport last night. Is that common? What if I want to travel to Egypt or something?"

"Yes," said Jessie, "They keep our passports but they give them back when it's time for holidays or if you want to travel. They have all the expatriate faculty documents. You don't need to worry about it; it'll be safe in the Dean's Office."

"Did Betsy mention who lived in your room before," questioned Amy.

"No, she hasn't talked much to me except to tell me to avoid drinking the faucet water," replied Elizabeth. "I did wonder why Betsy had no roommate but I didn't get a chance to ask her."

"Yes, well, all unmarried women under age fifty are required to have a roommate here, even foreigners." Amy went on to explain, "Her former roommate, also a nurse, left us holding the bag when she got us to cover her two months salary bond required so she could go off at pilgrimage time to visit India. She never came back and never paid us back."

"Whatever happened to her?" asked Elizabeth.

"We heard that she took a job teaching in a Indian nursing school. We tried to contact her through the embassy but got no where."

When she returned downstairs to her own flat, she heard Ina talking on the telephone so she went back to the dining room area to greet her just as she was hanging up. "Well,

I guess you met Jessie Edwards and Amy Burch. I do my best to stay out of their way," said Ina.

Elizabeth waited for her to say more but she did not. So Elizabeth simply tucked this little comment away to ponder till she knew the lay of the land better. Right now, she didn't want to focus on gossip and negativity. Certainly, she had met several nurses who did not get along with their bosses, but working in a hospital unit, you learn to overcome most of that so you don't shortchange you patients, she reminded herself.

CHAPTER 5

CHOP SQUARE!

Good as their words, Jessie and Amy appeared at the door at 7:30 AM the next morning. They needed to start early as the mid-day heat in August became unbearable quickly. Both women had black *abayas* over their long sleeves and long skirts. Their faces and heads were uncovered. Jessie held out an *abaya* to Elizabeth saying, "You can borrow this one until you buy your own."

It was a little disorienting to have this day be like Saturday when it was really only Thursday. Because she had arrived in the middle of the night, and the flat had no windows, only a balcony is Ina's room, this was her first real look at her surroundings. Outside the walls of the compound, they walked along the cement sidewalk which was about fifteen inches above the paved street. Elizabeth could feel the heat of the cement through her leather-soled sandals. She wore one of the two long skirts she had brought with her. She walked between Amy and Jessie. They seemed protective of her.

"Let's take a taxi instead of waiting for the bus," said Jessie. Since there will be three of us, nobody can accuse us of being alone with a man. You already know about that rule don't you, Elizabeth?"

"I read the suggestion sheet sent from the Houston Consulate about what to wear and how to act, more or less.

But I knew I'd have to learn most of these rules when I got here. Please tell me anything you think I need to know," she replied.

As they stood at the high curb, alert to the passing traffic, Elizabeth saw that the buildings all around were enclosed in high walls, making it difficult to try to discover their functions as most had no number or name on the wall by the gate, not even names in Arabic. Towering over the area was the Riyadh city water tower which had the shape of a mushroom with painted vertical stripes. There were a few palm trees in the median of the street, but otherwise the color of the landscape was predominantly the dun color of the compound walls.

Cars raced by in the street, pulling up to the stoplight at the intersection with no sense of order. They all seemed to be nosing slowly into the intersection even before the light changed. Elizabeth could see that they drove on the same side of the street as they did in California but it mattered little to her as she knew she would not be driving here due to the prohibition on women drivers. She guessed she must have been too tired to notice which side they drove on during the trip from the airport. They crossed the street to be on the side where the taxi would be heading toward the *souq*.

The late August sun was already beating down on their black *abayas*, even at 7:30 in the morning. "I brought a bottle of water for you," Jessie said. "I figured you probably weren't in the habit of carrying one with you but you'll need to do it here." She brought out a plastic bottle and handed it to Elizabeth as a Mitsubishi 929 taxi pulled up to the curb.

Amy got into the front passenger seat of the taxi. She said something to the driver in Arabic. Jessie held the backseat door for Elizabeth and slid in after her, clutching her *abaya.* Elizabeth was fascinated to watch what passed by as they sped and zigzagged between other cars. The driver wore a rather dirty formerly white *thobe,* a robe and green checkered *ghutra* on his head. He had on sunglasses which reminded Elizabeth to find hers in the bottom of her purse. He drove with abandon, apparently adhering to the much spoken saying *En Sha Allah* 'If God Wills It.' Elizabeth came to know this saying well, as it was used whenever discussing anything in the future. She felt that the driver must indeed be trusting *Allah* as he seemed to look neither to the left or right. His *ghutra* cut off his peripheral vision. She decided she must adopt the same attitude and trust that they would arrive at the *souq* intact.

She was aware as she watched the scenery pass by the car window that there were no women on the street until they approached the square in front of the *souq.* Then she saw several pairs of completely black clad women. Elizabeth wondered how they could stand to be all covered in black without even their faces free to the breeze. The archway into the *souq* was welcoming shade from the sun which reached through her clothes even in the thirty feet walk from the taxi to the archway.

It took several moments for her eyes to adjust from the bright desert sunlight to the dim light of the *souq* corridor. When she could finally see her surroundings, the first thing she saw as well as smelled was a woman seated on the ground behind a dozen half-barrels of spices. The spicy aroma in the heat was almost overpowering.

Jessie said, "I need to go order a bracelet to take to my

daughter when I meet her in Egypt at *hajj*. Amy, you take Elizabeth to the *abaya* booths, OK?"

"Sure, I'll be glad to help her find the right *abaya*. Let's meet at *shawarma* booth near the other end of the souq, OK?" said Amy.

As they advanced further into the dimly lit corridor, passing women wearing both the *niqab* with eye slits and others with completely covered faces, she saw on her left a booth with brass *hookahs* of various sizes with beautifully woven cord covers leading up from the water tank to the mouth piece. The proprietor was a handsome bearded man with his brown checkered *ghutra* wrapped like a turban around his head. He was demonstrating a tall gleaming water-pipe to a male customer. Nonetheless, she saw his eyes following her uncovered face. Apparently a new female in the *souq* was rare enough that he was aware of it as he did not glance at Amy.

A few yards further on the other side of the corridor there were piles of brightly colored carpets, all different sizes. Elizabeth was immediately drawn toward these gem-colored rugs. This proprietor gestured to her to come in after he saw the eager look on her face. She smiled and shook her head "No" as she knew she needed to get settled before she bought anything except her own foam mattress. However, the fluffy gray cat seated on a tall pile of carpets toward the back of the booth reminded her of her own cat in Los Angeles for which she had to find a home while she was away.

Eventually, they made it to the end of the corridor and found a small table in the covered area just outside. Amy went to the counter and ordered coffee which a boy brought to the table on a tray with three small cups and an Arabic brass coffee server, a *dallah*. "I asked for three cups because I know that Jessie will want a cup when she comes," Amy said as she poured coffee into two of the tiny cups. The coffee tasted wonderfully rich, much better than the thin stuff at home or what she made in her percolator.

Jessie arrived and pulled a small white plastic bag with Arabic lettering out of her purse and showed off the bracelet she purchased. "I saw exactly the bracelet I wanted for Jenna so I went ahead and bought it rather than order one," said Jessie as she sat down. She held up a bright gold bangle with a leaf garland pattern molded on it. She waited for their admiration before asking, "Do you mind walking back through the *souq* to Chop Square? I want to stop and buy some cardamom from the spice lady. Did you find an *abaya*?"

Elizabeth indicated the negative as she nodded "no." She had been so excited by all the new sights, sounds and smells, she had forgotten as apparently had Amy.

Elizabeth was more than eager to walk back through the thrilling, colorful booths lining the corridor. She was already anticipating covering her floor with colorful carpets. As the three women emerged at the other end of the *souq*, Elizabeth saw several Asian-looking men pushing brooms in the square. Their brooms pushed dust, food wrappers and plastic water bottles toward some garbage cans on the paving near a truck.

"Do they do this everyday?" asked Elizabeth nodding toward the sweepers?

"No, they usually do it on Thursday to prepare for Friday.

After prayer in the mosque tomorrow, they must be having an execution here in this square," explained Jessie. "That's why this square is called Chop Square. This is where they have most of the executions after Friday prayers." Jessie was phlegmatic as she explained this.

Elizabeth was appalled and somewhat surprised to meet this aspect of Saudi Arabia so soon after her arrival. She had read of this in the State Department book but it had little reality until this moment. Her impulse was to leave quickly but she didn't know how to get home. So she submissively followed her new colleagues as they headed across the square to another smaller doorway where Jessie said there was another *abaya souq*.

This *souq* was more like a department store but without the manikins in the show windows, since Saudi Islam forbids images, thus no windows full of statues wearing clothes.

Chapter 6

Sabbath in Riyadh

The next morning Elizabeth slept in despite the hardness of the floor under the foam mattress and began to recover from the jet lag which she was informed by Jessie, was always more severe when you flew east toward the sun rather than west with the sun. She had not seen her roommate, neither when she returned from the *souq* in the late afternoon, nor the next morning as she bathed and groomed herself, and figured out how to make coffee. She ate a granola bar for breakfast as she had packed some just in case, as she had anticipated, that she might not be able to find food immediately upon arrival. There might be no restaurant or grocery store nearby and she would need time to find them.

Jessie and Amy had promised her when they left her the night before, that they would bring her along to the Riyadh International Christian Fellowship so she could meet some other Westerners. Good as their word, at nine-thirty, there was a knock on the door and since her room was close by, she immediately opened it and invited them in. They stood in the hallway of the flat. They were obviously not comfortable in this flat. This was something to explore for the future but for now, Elizabeth gathered her *abaya* about her and slung her purse over her shoulder struggling to discourage it from dragging her *abaya* off her shoulder. She realized it would take some time to be comfortable with the black cloak. Amy lent her a headscarf and helped her wrap it over her hair. The same little man she had seen when Mr. Rahman first brought her in the building was sitting on a short stool inside the small room by the entrance inside the lobby. Jessie whispered in an aside as they passed him, "We call him 'the watchdog.'"

When they walked out of the compound unto the sidewalk, the heat pounded her through the *abaya* and headscarf. This heat was much fiercer than any she had ever felt in Southern California.

"Chuck Toiler is going to pick us up," explained Jessie. She led the way to the cut-out parking space near the ambulance ramp into the hospital. There was a bench there apparently placed for those waiting for their ride. Very shortly a big American Buick drove into the space and the driver jumped out and came around opening each door that he passed. Jessie got into the front passenger seat and Amy gestured to Elizabeth to take the seat behind the driver. He had moved more quickly than his appearance would have attested about his age. His hair was iron gray and his skin was like leather. But his agility belied his appearance. He ran around again closing the doors after each woman got in. "How you ladies?" he drawled as he pulled away and out of the hospital compound.

Jessie turned around and introduced him as they nosed their way into the traffic. Then she went on to explain that they were driving on Airport Road, a main street through the city. "That's what the expats call it," she said. "Chuck works for Lockheed and so he picks us up and drives right through their gate. They just look at the sticker on the car and we don't even have to stop so they can see his license."

The air-conditioning in the Buick was welcome even

though they had been on that bench only a few minutes. It had been long enough for Elizabeth to feel the dry heat of the desert sun. The fronds of the palms moved in the air making one think the wind was blowing, but she had felt no breeze while waiting on the bench. Perhaps the walls blocked the breeze, she thought.

The Lockheed Compound was well marked and not far off Airport Road. The sign said L-160. Was Lockheed as big as that number indicated? As predicted by Jessie, they glided by the guard hut without even stopping. There were a number of cars parked around a building marked Recreation Hall. There was a rush of cold air as Chuck opened the door and gallantly stood aside to let the women enter first. The room was rather plain but there was a pulpit at the front and a simple altar with a tan silk cloth under a simple brass cross. Though Elizabeth considered herself an agnostic where religion was concerned, she had no qualms about attending other peoples' churches or worship services. A woman in a long aqua print dress sat behind a keyboard at one side near the front. She was playing 'The Old Rugged Cross' as people took their seats. The minister stepped in from an anteroom where he had apparently been donning his robe. The music drifted off as he raised his eyes to heaven and began to pray, "Lord, hear our prayers, as we foreigners in a foreign land come to worship you. We seek your guidance as we struggle to learn how to be good guests in Riyadh. We find strange customs all around us and seek to better understand our hosts and their ways. Please help us keep our Christian truths as we go about finding our way in these unaccustomed surroundings. Help us to be the best disciples of your love so our hosts will see your message in our works. Amen!"

Elizabeth recognized his accent as the same kind she heard in Southern California, the accent she equated with television, the language of newscasters and public speakers from the home state. She thought of it as having no accent compared to southerners she had met here, Jessie, Amy and Chuck.

The keyboard woman hit the keys with 'Standing on the Promises' as the congregation stood and joined in. Apparently, they all knew the verses. Then Elizabeth realized that the hymn number was written on the chalkboard near the pulpit. Amy shoved a hymnal open to that hymn into her hands. The singing was very animated but since Elizabeth seldom attended any worship service, she had little to compare it too. However, both her companions seemed to know the words.

Rev. Davis gave a short homily on "Foreigners in a Foreign Land." He had several common sense rules under laid with ideas of God's promises to sustain folks. Another hymn, the Lord's Prayer, announcements of members who had gone home or new members who had joined, announcement of the drama group's play practice and where to sign up, announcement of the next prison visit and whom to contact, another prayer and they were up singing the 'Doxology.'

People flowed out of the folding chairs toward the kitchenette counter where coffee and cookies were being served. Elizabeth noticed that there were many fewer women than men in this congregation. A few of the men even looked as though they were Middle Eastern. Later she learned that some Coptic Christians from Egypt attended these services.Elizabeth took her coffee and cookie to the side as Amy and Jessie became engaged in conversations with people they apparently knew. She stood with her back to the wall, sipping coffee and watching the whole group. As she scanned the room, she met the eyes of an attractive iron gray haired man watching her as he pretended to converse with another man. She quickly averted her eyes as she felt unsure of the etiquette of this group. Besides, she did not come here to meet men. And the State Department book had been very explicit about avoiding breaking Saudi laws regarding sexual relationships.

Finally, she saw Chuck approaching Jessie and Amy who always seemed to be together. He turned and pointed toward Elizabeth and Jessie made a 'Come here' gesture with her hand. They all moved toward the door. Elizabeth was glad they had not tried to introduce her to anyone as she knew she'd never remember names at this time.

"How about some brunch at the International Hotel restaurant?" Chuck asked. "And then how about I drive you three around the city so Elizabeth can see the sights?" He said this laughing as if it were irony or sarcasm.

"Well, I think that's a good idea, a good way to introduce Elizabeth to her new home," affirmed Jessie. Amy nodded her agreement, though Elizabeth felt a nap might feel good right now. The car air-conditioning lulled her so she simply nodded affirmatively. Maybe the coffee at brunch might give her energy. The coffee at the Riyadh International Fellowship had certainly not.

The restaurant in the hotel was rather grand with tables end-to-end several yards long covered with platters of food; cut-up fruits, bananas, grapes, small pastries, meatballs, kebabs, stuffed grape-leaves, baklava, juices, coffee, teas, eggs of several varieties such as deviled, marinated peeled boiled eggs, stuffed dates and more. Chuck ushered them to a table near the glass enclosed patio. The patio was covered with what seemed like stained glass so it partially shielded the space from the bright noonday sun.

"Well, what did you think of the worship service?" asked Amy as the women deposited their purses and *abayas* on their chairs and turned toward the buffet line.

"To tell the truth, I was so busy trying to observe and do things properly that I hardly had time to form an opinion. But I'm glad I was there," Elizabeth answered in order not to display her lack of enthusiasm for organized worship. As they proceeded through the line, she was encouraged to try this or that food. Other conversation stopped as they focused on what was on the platters.

Back at the table, Chuck began between mouthfuls to recite names of possible driving destinations. Planning their upcoming outing took up all the conversation during the meal. Elizabeth noticed that a few of the folks she had seen at the Riyadh International Christian Fellowship had also found their way to this hotel. One couple came over to their table as they were finishing their meal. The middle-aged woman asked, "And who do we have here, Jessie?"

After introductions, the couple departed, the woman saying "May God bless you as you start classes." As they moved away, Jessie leaned in to tell Elizabeth more about this couple who came from Washington D.C. as consultants from the US Treasury Department to the Saudi Ministry of Finance. Apparently Mrs. Shaker was a pillar of the International Fellowship and chaired the committee on visitation to Christians incarcerated in Riyadh jails. She had tried to get Jessie and Amy to join her on a visit to the women's prison, but they were working women and had enough to do without adding prison visitations. Mrs. Shaker, on the other hand, had no obligations except their villa in the compound reserved for US government consultants' families. She found the prison visitation exciting besides making her feel she was doing important work like her husband.

"Be careful around her," said Amy, "or she'll have you on her prison visitation committee."

"I won't take on anything like that until I figure out my work load here in the University," replied Elizabeth.

Chuck was as good as his word, touring them around the new embassy section, the exterior walls of the National Saudia University for Girls and the newest streets furthest from Airport Road. It provided a more expansive view of the city and its desert surroundings.

CHAPTER 7

CAMPUS

Friday evening, following prayers in Arabic on the fifteen minutes of English TV news that Elizabeth watched in the flat of Jessie and Amy, as she had no access to TV in her own flat, they announced the execution of two Filipino men for drug dealing. Though they did not show the actual execution, they showed photographs of the two men. The three women sat immobile after the announcement. Even Amy and Jessie, who had been here two years already, seemed stunned. Elizabeth surmised it was their proximity the day before to the men sweeping Chop Square that affected them so.

"Let me make us some tea," offered Amy as she arose and went to their kitchen. Apparently she had determined that they all needed a few moments to assimilate this news. Their prediction of the day before had indeed been correct.

With regular mugs in their laps this time, the two women who had been in Riyadh longer attempted to reassure Elizabeth that beheadings were an infrequent occurrence despite telling her yesterday that the sweepers were preparing for an execution. Jessie finally redirected their conversation to plans for going to the University the next morning. They agreed to meet near the indoor hut of the little watchdog-man by the front door. It was air-conditioned there in the lobby thus saving them a few minutes of the August desert heat.

Saturday morning, which was like Monday morning at home in the States, they crossed the busy intersection with the car hoods all pushing into the crosswalk. They awaited the bus at the same spot where they had hailed the cab on Thursday morning.

"We'll be sitting in the women's section in the back," explained Jessie. "It used to be in the front, but they realized that all the men just peeped around the partitions to see the women, so they reversed it. Now women sit in the back so the men can't see them." She used her *abaya* clad elbow to point to the line of men standing a few yards away to their right on the sidewalk.

At that moment, the bus pulled up and the doors to both sections opened simultaneously. Jessie and Amy stepped up the rather deep cutout steps over the back wheels and found a seat along the upholstered back bench at the rear. Fortunately there was room for Elizabeth to sit right beside them. There was only one other *abaya*-clad woman in this back section which looked like it would hold at the maximum ten seated women. If more than that ascended, they would have to stand in the aisle. Elizabeth realized that she could see around the Formica covered partitions and the men's section on the other side was almost completely full with men standing in the aisle grasping the overhead bar. One or two faced back toward the women's section seeming to try to see who was hidden behind the partition. Elizabeth stared back curiously. Eventually, one of the men turned away as if in shame. The other, bolder, just kept on eyeing them around the five inch space between the wall of the bus and the partition.

The bus stopped and they descended on a street which was unremarkable as all the high walls looked alike. Had she tried to find the campus herself, Elizabeth knew she would have been unable to do it, even if she had the address. Every street looked alike to her. It would take her a while to be able to distinguish one street from another, one building from another since they all seemed to be hidden behind high tan walls.

She followed Jessie and Amy though a gate where another robed male gatekeeper eyed every woman entering. Many of them had their faces covered. Immediately inside the wooden gates was another wall which Jessie explained was to keep men from looking inside at the women when the outside gates were open. Immediately, the new National Saudia University for Girl's Administration Building was on the left. There were several other separate buildings behind inside this compound. Beside the huge potted palm trees on the marble columned portico leading up to the brass framed double doors, there was no greenery or landscaping visible except one small brick-bordered flower bed with a small fountain which must have been rigorously tended in this desert heat. It was a riot of colorful flowers.

The buildings were labeled but in Arabic. Elizabeth followed Amy and Jessie into a building which was indistinguishable from the others. As they mounted the stairs, Jessie explained that they shared this building with the biology department. Most of the nursing students had come to them through the biology department and so the administration felt it was common sense to put nursing there, too. The women's medical school was on yet another campus nearer the hospital. Jessie had her own office as she was the Chair of the Nursing Department though she taught some classes as well. Amy had another office which she shared with one of the Egyptian teachers named Samia.

Jessie went right to work on her administrative preparations for the start of the upcoming semester. She assigned Amy the task of touring Elizabeth first around the department and then around the campus. There were faculty members from several other Middle Eastern countries; Turkey, Egypt and Pakistan. "Most of the other nursing faculty members are Muslim. They will arrive tomorrow as they don't usually travel on the Sabbath or at least that's their excuse. They're flying in today," Amy explained. "We'll have a faculty meeting tomorrow after they get here."

Elizabeth was assigned to share an office with Nour, another Egyptian nurse. The office they would share was an etched glass-walled space of approximately ten feet by sixteen feet with a desk and chair against the one solid wall on either end. Both desktops were bare. Either would be adequate for preparing her lessons. She had brought nothing with her to put in her desk yet. Elizabeth decided that she would carry a few of her chosen textbooks with her on the bus each day until she had them all here in the office. Amy suggested, "You could just bring them in a taxi all at once."

"Oh, I just don't feel confident traveling by myself from the flat to here yet. I think I'll just bring a few at a time on the bus as I'd probably get lost trying to tell a cab driver how to get here," Elizabeth explained.

"Well, we could get Amal, the secretary to write the name of the University on a paper for you to show to the cab drive. Of course, not all the cab drivers can read. So maybe it is better to just bring a few each day and ride the bus with us."

Amal's desk was in a space outside Jessie's office. Amy introduced them saying, "Amal, this is Elizabeth Adams, you know the new teacher from California. I am just showing her around the school now but I am sure she will have questions for you sometime."

Amal looked very much the professional secretary, dressed in a silky peach colored long-sleeved blouse, gold earrings and necklace and slim black floor length skirt. Her dark hair was styled into a perfect shoulder length pageboy. She stood up from her desk which held a typewriter and telephone, plus a yellow legal sized tablet from which she was apparently typing something. She reached out to shake Elizabeth's hand saying, "Welcome" in accented English.

When Amy showed her the nursing anatomy laboratory, Elizabeth was amazed to see almost every type of plastic anatomical model for both male and female bodies. On one cupboard counter along a twenty foot wall, they had a dozen female bodies with fetuses in every stage of gestation. And the uteruses were removable. She could see that no money had been spared in outfitting this nursing laboratory. It was a very spacious room connected to another laboratory room with several patient beds containing plastic patient models covered with sheets. The two laboratories had a folding plastic curtain which could be used to separate them. Elizabeth was over whelmed as she thought back to some of the skimpy measures she had had to observe with her students in Southern California.

"How many students are usually in each class?" she asked.

"Well the senior class has only one student. The junior class has three," replied Amy.

Elizabeth's eyes fluttered as she assimilated this. Her classes in California had averaged between twenty and twenty five students each semester. This would be almost like tutoring rather than classroom teaching.

Since the students did not actually start classes until the following Saturday, like Monday at home, Elizabeth decided to read through the syllabus the previous med/surg teacher had used and then make one of her own. She would be doing a beginners med/surg class for the juniors and an advanced class for the one senior. It seemed like overkill to make a complicated syllabus for just one student, but who was she to argue with this plethora, this superabundance of resources to prepare for one senior student and for the three beginners.

She asked Amal, the secretary if there was another typewriter in the department besides the one on her desk. During the tour, she had noticed that there were no typewriters on other faculty desks as there were in her nursing school in California where faculty often did their own typing. She had shipped her own portable typewriter, sewing machine and autoharp from California but the instruction sheet she had received in Houston explaining what to do to prepare for Riyadh, had said it might take up to a month to receive such shipments. She had considered just storing them as she did not know whether or not she might be here longer than one year, and she thought she could survive that long without them, but had decided in the interest of having some familiar tools around her, to send them on ahead.

Amal replied in her accented English, "This the only typewriter in department. You use it while I have tea. Most faculty print and I type." Her stiff smile told Elizabeth that she did not share her typewriter easily.

It was at this moment that Elizabeth realized she was the only one in this department besides Amal who typed. So for now, she would have to hand-print out her syllabus to be typed by Amal.

Chapter 8

Desert Ramblers

It was a relief to see the bus coming as they stood on the corner in the afternoon desert heat. On the way home on the air-conditioned bus at 1:00 PM, Amy invited Elizabeth to the Sunday evening Desert Ramblers meeting tomorrow evening which was to be held in the auditorium of the College of Dentistry. It was within walking distance of their flats. Amy said it would be a good introduction to what Westerners did for fun in Saudi.

Ina Brooks was already home when Elizabeth unlocked the door. She could hear music coming from back in Ina's bedroom. Elizabeth had not seen her at the office all day though Amy had shown her which office Ina shared with one of the Egyptian faculty.

Elizabeth headed for the kitchen and to the refrigerator to drink some cold water. She promised herself she would save the next plastic water bottle she got her hands on so she could remember to always carry water in her purse. Dehydration was one of the main enemies of desert living she had heard several times already.

Though she had been here half a week, so that her jet-lag was somewhat resolved, the enforced afternoon rest time was very welcome. This Saudi custom of taking several hours off each afternoon for a long nap was something Elizabeth would come to value. Jessie had explained to her on the bus that men have to go back to the office at 4 PM and work a couple hours before going home to dinner about 7 PM. Women on the other hand, being considered the weaker sex, were excused from evening work. When they left the campus of National Saudia University for Girls at 1 PM, they were done for the day. However, it also meant that they must contrive to get everything that needed to be taught into the hours between 8 AM and 1 PM.

The following morning, which was Sunday, Elizabeth discovered that her office mate, Nour, had already arrived. Since Elizabeth had not brought any of her professional books the day before, she had not left anything on either desk to indicated possession. Nour had claimed the desk nearer the door which was fine with Elizabeth. She realized she would have more privacy by working at the desk at the far end of their narrow office. She shook Nour's rather limp hand as she introduced herself.

Nour, a name which Elizabeth later learned meant light, did have a sunny personality. She was a little below medium height compared to the American nurses. Her rich brown hair was worn drawn back into a knot at her neck. She wore a traditional Egyptian *galabaya*. The golden color set off her golden skin and hazel eyes. Nour turned back to her work.

In the corner of the glass walled office, Elizabeth realized there was another piece of furniture, a pole style hat rack which held Nour's *abaya*. It sat in the corner behind Elizabeth's desk chair. Elizabeth hung her own *abaya* on another of the hooks and sat down. "What courses do you teach?" she asked Nour as she pulled open the various drawers and discovered a box of pens, paper clips, cello tape, scissors and a stack of yellow legal size tablets.

"I usually teach the first laboratory course on ward skills, like bed bathes, wound care, hand washing, disinfecting the area, those things. What do you teach?" Nour replied in her very slightly accented English while turning in her chair to face Elizabeth.

Elizabeth explained what she had taught in California and how she expected she would be teaching the same thing here but she would teach whatever classes she was assigned. "Are you here on your own? And do you live in the same building we live in by the hospital?"

"No, I am here with my husband and daughter. My husband is an engineer. I got my job here after we arrived. We live in the compound of my husband's company," Nour explained. "My husband brings me to the university on his way to work."

Elizabeth knew from this easy first meeting that she and Nour were going to be friends despite the limp handshake.

~~~

That evening after a nice afternoon nap, she dined with Jessie and Amy before they walked to the School of Dentistry. The temperature had diminished perhaps twenty degrees Fahrenheit since they had gotten off the bus at 1:30 PM. The dental building, like the nursing lab, seemed to have the most up-to-date of everything needed to teach. The auditorium looked like it would hold perhaps 200 people in the seats on different levels sloping down to the front. When they entered, there were already perhaps
~~~

thirty people clustered in the rows near the podium. Most of them were men with five or six women scattered in between. Some hand drawn maps on brown butcher paper had been hung over the chalkboard behind the podium.

A middle aged white man with an Australian accent walked to the podium and introduced the speaker and his wife, Dr. and Mrs. Clough, who were going to describe their recent tour of *Wadi Al Miyah* in the Eastern Province.

Dr. Clough walked to the podium while Mrs. Clough simply stood in her front row seat and turned and waved at the audience which was slowly enlarging. There were nearly fifty people as Dr. Clough took the podium. His Scottish burr was immediately apparent. "Last year, Mrs. Clough and I and another British couple and a couple British Army lads drove out to *Wadi Al Miyah* to explore. My wife made these maps of our trip. I will be referring to them as I describe our adventure." He gestured toward the butcher-paper maps.

Elizabeth took her attention away from the speaker and his maps to look at the other audience members. The three nursing faculty were sitting in the third row. She had to turn her head only slightly to see everyone present. She counted the women present and including Amy, Jessie and herself; there were eight women and forty nine men. They were all in western dress except the women all wore long dresses or skirts. The men were in shirt sleeves as was even the speaker. There were no men in Saudi dress in the audience. Curious, thought Elizabeth. Later she realized that most Riyadh Saudis distanced themselves from their Bedouin heritage. Trekking into the desert just reminded them.

Dr. Clough recounted their early morning departure with their teenage children in their Landrover. He described their first campsite and pointed it out on the map. He told of the deserted settlements of the local *Awazim* tribe and the wells surrounding each village. They met herds of camels, donkeys, desert flowers, and looked for pottery shards, before the five hour drive back to Riyadh. At the conclusion, there was a question and answer session. Attendees asked esoteric questions about stone work in the water wells, genus and species of the flowers, and the hazards of hiking up the escarpment.

As the audience clapped their approval of the presentation, Elizabeth again took the opportunity to look at the other audience members. It seemed that most of the other women here were wives of men in the audience. They seemed to know each other and to know Amy and Jessie. As the other two nurses introduced her around, a tall rugged man in an American Army uniform inserted himself and asked to be introduced. She realized he was the same attractive iron gray haired man who had been watching her at the Riyadh International Christian Fellowship on Friday. His name was David Nelson.

As they conversed, she realized that some of the other single men had clustered around the three single women. She tried not to be distracted from her conversation with David Nelson as the other men were obviously interested in her though they talked to Amy and Jessie.

David said, "There's going to be an excursion out to look for desert diamonds next Thursday. We're planning to caravan out there. Could I interest you in joining us? I'm driving my American Army jeep and I've got extra seats."

"What are desert diamonds?" asked Elizabeth as she tried to delay for time to get the attention of Amy or Jessie to see if they thought this was a good idea or might even want to join such an outing. She still felt somewhat uncertain about what was allowed between men and women here.

"They are a quartz sometimes called *Qaisumah* diamonds but they are really good quality. They can be cut to look like diamonds," he explained.

Being unable to subtly get the attention of Jessie or Amy, Elizabeth laid her hand on Jessie's arm. "Is there any reason we can't join David and the others for the desert diamond outing next Thursday?"

Jessie dragged her attention away from a conversation with another clean shaven iron grey haired American dressed in denim jeans and a plaid shirt. Jessie replied, "I think that sounds like a good trip for your first outing since its not overnight. We'd love to be included." Later Jessie explained it was good to be friendly with most of these men as they could drive you places where buses did not go and being alone in a taxi with an Arab driver was not always safe.

Elizabeth turned back to David Nelson to confirm their intention to join the desert diamond outing. "It will be a good time to join you before our students arrive next Saturday to start classes. Jessie and Amy will probably join us, too. Do you have room for all of us?"

"Oh, yes, the more the merrier, especially with three women here in the land of hidden women. Besides if there are three of you, it will be legal." David laughed as he said this. "Do you have a telephone yet?"

"Not yet, but you could call and leave a message for me at the nursing department. What should I wear? Do I have to wear a dress or could I wear my jeans? I expect I'll need to wear my *abaya* until we get away from the city," Elizabeth said thoughtfully.

"Oh, definitely wear jeans if you brought them. Be sure to bring a hat. And yes, wear an *abaya* till we get out of town. If we go through a village where they have a police checkpoint, you'll need it too." David wrote down her office number. "I'll call you to let you know what time. You know what an American Army jeep looks like, yes?" He smiled at his own joke.

Chapter 9

Ahlan wa Sahlan

Her first class with the three juniors was delayed in starting as the third student was half-an-hour late. Elizabeth was conflicted about how she should respond as she had already in her week in Riyadh heard the saying 'Saudi Time' more than once. She had already welcomed the two who had been on-time; Amina, and Fairuz. This third student introduced herself as Mouna. Later Elizabeth would learn the meaning of their names. Mouna which meant wish or desire would always protest that it was her desire to be on time but the driver was late or that the driver took a wrong turn or the driver was late in picking her up. This last excuse was probably fabricated as most drivers lived in the compounds surrounding the villas of the family of these girls. Elizabeth learned this later.

The classroom was the same size as a regular school room in the USA, approximately thirty-five feet by thirty-five feet. They sat in a small cluster near the front of the room. Elizabeth dragged a student chair around to be closer to face the three students. After introducing herself, she began speaking slowly about her previous work places. In order to discover their English speaking abilities, she asked student each to stand to introduce herself. She wrote three things on the chalkboard that she wished them to include in their introduction; their full name including their family name, how many people were in their families and why they wanted to be a nurse. "Amina, please start since your name starts with the first letter in the English alphabet," she said slowly.

Amina spoke slowly but seemed prepared to answer in English. She wore a white embroidered silk blouse and pencil slim long black skirt. Though she seemed shy in standing before her peers, it was with grace that she moved in her tight long skirt. "My name is Amina Khoury. In my family, we have Grandmother, Father, Mother, sister Fatima, brother Khalid, sister Yasmina, sister Khadijah, sister Hafsa and Baby Yacob." She counted them off on her fingers as she named them. "Oh, also I forgot Aunt Maymunah. I want to be a nurse because I watched the nurse care for Grandmother in the hospital. She was so kind."

After each girl had performed the same exercise, Elizabeth realized that though they had been able to answer in understandable English, they would be going very slowly through her syllabus. She wondered if she would be able to progress more than halfway through during this first introductory class.

The syllabi were passed to each student. Elizabeth led them through a discussion of what was expected of them for each session with page numbers for readings in their textbooks which had not arrived yet. She had had Amal, the secretary, make copies of the first chapters which she now distributed to the three students. Hopefully, the books, a shipment containing textbooks for every class, which had been ordered from the USA by Jessie, last June, would arrive by the time they had moved through these photocopied pages.

She spent most of the time during this first session getting to know these young women. Fairuz, which means turquoise in Arabic as Elizabeth learned later, was dressed completely in that color. The garment was a silky looking dress with cloth covered matching buttons completely down the front. The color set off the olive skin, dark eyes and long hair and precisely plucked eyebrows. Fairuz Maloof also wore turquoise and gold dangling earrings and a matching necklace. She was stunning, small and slim, well able to wear this brilliant outfit. On her feet she wore matching high heels which added an inch or two to her height. Elizabeth thought how sad it was she had to hide it under the *abaya* which lay on the chair beside her along with her face veil and *hijab*, hair cover.

Fairuz had decided upon the nursing career when her English score was not high enough to provide her admittance to the female medical school. She came from a family of male doctors so this situation was difficult for her. However, Elizabeth did not learn this until much later as on this first day, Fairuz simply listed her four brothers and one sister. Elizabeth wondered if such a beautifully dressed woman would relish the duties of the beginning nurse.

Mouna, unlike the other two young women, had medium brown hair pulled back into a chignon. She was a little larger boned than the other two women. Her face was round and full with an unremarkable nose compared to the classic Arabic narrow mildly hooked noses of the other two. She did not seem as shy about standing in front of her peers and her new teacher. Mouna's English language was slightly more fluid than the other two. She explained that her mother was Syrian. Her father had gone to Syria to meet her before they married. Mouna's Syrian grandfather had been an import/export business man dealing mostly in jewelry. He had met her father, also an importer/exporter during a trip to Saudi Arabia and consequently invited him to Damascus to choose one of his seven daughters. Mouna wore a peach colored silky looking blouse and a brown gabardine skirt. She wore flat shoes as she was taller than the others and did not seem to need more height. Her golden jewelry was a good advertisement for her father's business. And her English was a tribute to the more international character of her father's business. She had one sister and one brother. She had met one of her Syrian aunts who was a nurse which Mouna learned when the aunt and husband came to make the pilgrimage to Mecca. The nurse-aunt became a sort of adolescent hero to her. This was why she wanted to enter this profession.

For her own first day with the students, Elizabeth had worn her only long skirt, a dark blue and white stripped cotton Guatemala cloth wrap-around, left over from her semi-hippy days. It seemed slightly more casual than any of the clothes worn by her students. She expected to make some other long skirts and dresses when she got her sewing machine. It would have been unwise, she felt, to buy long skirts in California until she saw what was worn in Saudi Arabia. The recommendation sheet she had been given in Houston, had just said "long to mid-calf skirts and long sleeved blouses." To add a little suggestion of professionalism for her first day, she wore the short white lab jacket with the nursing school patch that she had worn while teaching in the California community college. It made it easy to move from being a classroom teacher to being a supervising nurse when she took the students to a hospital or clinic. Also, it suggested a little distance between teacher and students which is what she wished here at the beginning.

Just as the class was about to wind down, as Elizabeth was reemphasizing their assignment for the next session, they heard the call to pray from the mosque across the street from the campus. Amina said, "It's time to pray," meanwhile watching Elizabeth to see her response. Fortunately for Elizabeth, Jessie had foreseen exactly this situation and had warned her to ward off this attempt to steal class-time by repeating Dean Ashwari who had proclaimed, "Do your prayers after class. Allah wants you to learn."

Apparently these students had attempted this ploy before and been rebuffed as they acquiesced easily when Elizabeth said "Wait till class is done." They took note of the pages assigned before the next session and did not stop to pray despite a pile of rolled-up prayer rugs in the back corner. They stood, wrapped their scarves over their hair, draped the face veils over their heads and donned their *abayas* before traipsing down the stairs. Mouna threw her face veil back over the top of the *abaya* rather than try to walk sightless down the stairs. The other two gripped the stair-rail as they peered through their veils and felt with their high heels to avoid stumbling.

As soon as Amy had finished teaching her class to the one senior, Ferdooz, Amy stuck her head in Nour and Elizabeth's office door. Nour had already departed as she did not start teaching until the following morning. Amy said, "Are you ready for lunch? I'll buy. There is a *falafel* stand near where we get off the bus. Let's see if Jessie's ready. By the way, you don't teach tomorrow do you? Why don't you come with me and Ferdooz to the 'well baby clinic' out in Ar Rimal. The university car and driver will take us. We won't have to take the bus. Ferdooz's parents would never let her do that."

They had the women's section of the bus to themselves at this hot hour. Jessie agreed with Amy's suggestion that Elizabeth accompany her to the Ar Rimal Clinic the next day. The *falafel* stand did not have a seating area. They each got a paper cone full of one inch round salted chickpea *falafel* dumplings which they sampled as they walked to the flats. The *falafels* were so hot that Elizabeth burned her lips on the first one. Jessie invited Elizabeth up to their flat to finish eating so they could see how her first day had gone.

The Ar Rimal Clinic junket had been Elizabeth's first experience in a real Saudi health care facility. Mr. Rahman picked them up on time outside the campus wall in the Pontiac. All three women and Ferdooz crowded into the back seat as it was really against the rules for a lone woman to sit with the driver and it was spacious enough. With a university employee, they did not want to appear to be breaking the rules. With the cab driver on Thursday, it had not mattered explained Jessie. Apparently, Mr. Rahman did not understand English, Elizabeth assumed as she listened. Their black *abayas* rubbed against each other but the air-conditioning in this new Pontiac was fierce enough that they didn't feel the outside heat at all.

As with all Saudi medical facilities, there were separate waiting rooms for males and females. This women's waiting room had chairs all around the walls, each with a black covered figure, each figure holding a baby or two. Some had their face veils thrown back as there were no men present. As the student-teacher group entered, wailing came from the other side of the wall where Elizabeth assumed the actual clinic was taking place. Amy found the nurse in charge who was a substantial mid-aged Egyptian wearing a white head scarf rather than the black Saudi one. She had on a floor length white nurse's uniform with an Arabic insignia on it. She ushered them into the clinic room where there were two other Egyptian nurses examining babies on sheet covered regular kitchen tables.

The senior student Ferdooz, immediately began a conversation with the examining nurses in Arabic language. Elizabeth found this a little frustrating as she could understand only a limited bit of what they said when they gestured or pointed. She decided she needed to know if they understood English so she might also converse with them and assess whether what they were saying fit with what she intended to teach. "I am Miss Adams. Do you speak English?"

All three nurses responded almost in unison, "Yes, I speak English." Then they laughed together as they realized what they had done. Later as Elizabeth talked with them individually, she realized that each one had a different level of understanding and of speaking English. But their procedure for examining the babies included everything she expected; hand washing, weighing, measuring, physical examination and some vaccinations, thus the wailing.

Chapter 10

Desert Diamonds

David Nelson had phoned her on Wednesday before Elizabeth, Amy and Jessie left the University to confirm that he would pick up the three nurses and their picnic basket in front of the medical personnel flats at 6 AM Thursday morning. There was a name on the front of the flats but it was in Arabic so all the Westerners just called it 'medical flats.'

This was Elizabeth's second weekend in the Kingdom. She felt pleased to be going on an outing outside the city so soon after she arrived. Her busy work and school life before in California had kept her from many adventures she craved.

David managed to arrange for Elizabeth to sit in the front bucket seat beside him and to have Jessie and Amy sit in the back seat. Plastic Jeri cans labeled gasoline and water were strapped to the back bumper. The jeep was not enclosed like the Oldsmobile sedan so the wind whipped their *abayas* around them as they finally left the city streets and headed out toward the desert, north east of Riyadh. It was too noisy with an open car for there to be much conversation. The vastness of the landscape through which they were riding, thorn trees, camels, herds of goats and Bedouin tents, was sufficient to keep them awake, even if the wind didn't. They did not even miss air-conditioning.

As the caravan topped the hill before the descent into the Al Qaisumah, David stopped their Jeep and asked Elizabeth to squeeze into the back seat too, as they would be going through a police check-point and all the women in the backseat would be protection for each other from being accused of being alone with a man to whom they were not related. Both Amy and Jessie, without instruction from him pulled their *abayas* back into place. Foreign women did not have to cover their faces but they knew it was easier all around if they conformed to the requirements, even out in the desert where rules were less strict. However, they also should not cover their faces with veils as they would be suspect if a foreign man was driving completely covered women. The police would ask why Saudi women were with a foreign man, which was also forbidden.

David had obviously been through this checkpoint before. As the women were moving around to be seated properly for the police, David pulled on a pair of kaki army slacks over his kaki shorts. Later he explained that he had once been hauled into a police station and questioned about wearing shorts. Consequently, he kept this pair of slacks in the jeep and put them on before ever every police station or checkpoint.

The women huddled in the back while David went into the police station. Apparently the officers were familiar with him as they did not even come out to the Jeep to see who was with him. "It's because I always have long pants on now," he explained.

They arrived at the desert diamond fields just after noon. It looked just like all the desert patches devoid of vegetation they had already passed. Elizabeth realized it was more barren than any California desert she had ever seen. "We can't see the desert diamonds in this light," David explained. "We'll be driving back in the dark because its only at dawn and dusk when they sparkle so you can see them in the sand."

Jessie and Amy had packed some peanut-butter sandwiches. People in the other vehicles in the caravan had brought fresh fruit, dates, boiled eggs, canned Pepsi, but nothing with alcohol, of course. There was no Coca Cola in Saudi Arabia as it was bottled in Israel and consequently could not be imported. And the Kingdom had recently outlawed even Near-Beer as the name was too similar to real beer. This was explained to Elizabeth during their sharing of lunches on a blanket laid out between the circled vehicles. Elizabeth also learned that while some foreigners made wine in their flats, they never took it out with them, lest they be caught with it and hauled into jail. Being from California where domestic wine was ubiquitous, this represented quite a change.

After the lunch remnants had been gathered back into the coolers and baskets, David asked Elizabeth, "Would you like to take a walk up toward that *jebel*? I've been up there before. It's a little cooler now." He gestured toward a nearby rock ridge.

She noticed that it was cooler and that the wind had picked up a little. "Do I have to wear my *abaya*?" she asked as she flung her bag over her should.

"Nah, you're not gonna meet any Saudi men out here

except *Bedu* and they are not nearly as strict as in the city. I'll stick an extra water bottle in my pack." He followed words with deeds and motioned for her to follow him.

"Let me tell Amy and Jessie where I'm going first," she responded and turned around to find them.

With just a brimmed cloth hat and no *abaya* over her jeans, Elizabeth remarked to David as they walked single file up a goat trail on the side of the *jebel*, "It doesn't seem too hot out here where there were no buildings to stop the wind." They passed acacia trees which were all nibbled evenly up to where camels could no longer reach, explained David. He occasionally gave her a hand when they came to particularly rough or narrow spots in the trail. She found this brief touch exciting in a way she'd almost forgotten about.

When they were able to walk beside each other, she began to query David about his life before Saudi Arabia.

"I was raised in New Haven, Connecticut and joined the Army right after college. It was when Viet Nam was just revving up. They took me into the officer corp. I'd actually been in ROTC in high school so nothing the Army threw at me surprised me much." He was walking ahead of Elizabeth as he told this part of his story. She was unable to see his expression but his voice was flat and uninflected.

"Did you have any brothers or sisters?" she asked. She hoped she did not sound like a nurse taking a patient history for the medical chart because she certainly didn't feel like that about him.

"Yes, I have one sister, younger than me a couple years. She's married and lives down nearer New York City in

Stamford, Connecticut."

Some instinct told her to ask about his own marital status since he looked to be about 40 years old and it would be unusual for an Army officer to still be single at that age. "How about you, have you ever been married?"

"Well, actually, I'm in the process of getting a divorce right now. That's kind of why I took this consulting job when the Army offered it to me. My almost ex-wife had started seeing this other guy while I was on maneuvers in California last year." He explained this without looking around to see her reaction though she could tell by the dropping of his shoulders that he was wary of her response.

It took Elizabeth a few seconds to think of a proper reply to this confession. "I suppose that is a hazard of the Army life. How long had you been married?"

"Well, I married her kind of on the rebound after I got home from Viet Nam in 1973. I'd been engaged to another woman before I went to Nam but she sent me a 'Dear John' letter before I got home. I was pretty devastated by that since we'd been dating since college, long before I went to Nam. I married Claire on the rebound."

"That sounds painful. Did you have any children?" said Elizabeth knowing that she sounded like a 'good' nurse as she said it though David did not seem to take it that way. She didn't want to pry but she wanted to know more about him. Keeping him talking kept him from asking her questions.

However, he recovered quickly from his apparent discomfort at explaining his life to her and asked, "And how about you? You look to be about thirty. I know I'm taking a risk guessing a woman's age but a lot of women who look about your age have been married, too."

"Yes, I'm divorced," she confessed though she did not elaborate. "I guess I have been too busy working and getting more education to think about that again."

As they finally reached the top of the *jebel* trail, the sun began to drop toward the west, toward Riyadh from where they had come that morning. "I guess we'd better head back down before it starts to get dark. We'll get down there just the right time to see the diamonds," David assured her. As they rounded a spot in the trail where their circle of caravan vehicles was not visible, David took her hand and pulled her a little closer and said, "I've really enjoyed this today, especially the hike and getting to know you a little better. Since you don't have a phone yet and it will be hard to get a hold of you, can we make another date now?"

"That sounds like a nice idea," she replied even though it in no way reflected the heightened feelings she felt for this man a they stood on the trail out of sight of the others.

"I know you went to church last Friday with Amy and Jessie and Chuck but how about if I pick you up tomorrow morning?"

Uncertain about whether it would be OK to go alone with a man here, Elizabeth asked, "Would it be OK? What I mean is would it be dangerous for me to go with you alone?"

"You sit in the back and there should be no problem. But if you are worried about it, talk to Jessie and Amy. They have both been here long enough to know the ins and outs of what's OK and what's not."

They reached the bottom of the *jebel* trail and headed across the flat desert where they could already see their fellow Desert Ramblers, hat-covered heads down looking for desert diamonds. When they reached the gem field, they joined in looking for the sparkles of the quartz pebbles.

Elizabeth was pleased to have found a couple specimens which others praised her for finding. Not everyone was so successful. Dr. Clough offered to take them to the gem cutter that cut his own stones whenever he found good ones. "Have you been to any of the hospitals or clinics, yet," he asked as they got ready to pile back into their vehicles. "If you come to visit King Faisel Hospital, be sure to stop in and say hello."

Chapter 11

Students

In the student laboratory at the School of Nursing, Elizabeth instructed her three juniors how to give injections by first injecting oranges until they felt comfortable with the procedure. Next they had to insert a needle into themselves and the final exercise before taking their new skill out to a clinic to practice on real patients was to insert needles and inject saline solution into each other. Elizabeth led them slowly through this step by step allowing them to feel the success of each action and to savor it a few days before inflicting the next trial on them. During these exercises, she began to know each student in an intense way she seldom had time for with her students in California.

Amina Khoury whose given name meant 'faithful and trustworthy' did not always show these characteristics as Elizabeth understood them. Amina was from a very religious family with a couple sisters named after the Prophet's wives. She lived in a family of mostly women, a grandmother, aunt and mother in addition to four sisters and two brothers. Her father worked in one of the ministries. He had never taken a second wife apparently because seven children and his sister and mother and one wife were all he could support on his government salary, though it was apparently quite generous. Additionally, his sister and his mother helped his wife convince him that another woman in the house would not be a happy situation.

Amina was the one who on the first day of class, had requested to stop class for prayer time. This little trick of attempted manipulation stuck in Elizabeth's mind as she got to know the girls. The experience of watching her maternal grandmother waste away in the hospital before her death had in some ways softened this aspect of Amina's personality. In a family of five girls and two boys, despite the perceived dominance of Saudi males, women ran the household. Her siblings held her in some respect for her ambition to be a nurse though that profession had been a slave's job up until Saudi Arabia's manumission of all slaves in 1961. These modern Saudi children were unaware of much of that history. And none of her siblings had her ambition to be a professional.

So Amina was both playful as well as caring and an example for her younger sisters. Elizabeth was watchful to see evidence of her living up to her name of "faithful." What does that mean to Muslims, she wondered.

Amina's slim five foot frame, almost always dressed in fashionable silks which would have been purchased in the mall, not the souq, could have been a model for what most young women her age wanted to look like without their *abayas*. But her *abayas* were all individualized with distinctive embroidery along the borders. Additionally, her silk *hijabs*, headscarves, were also decorated with special embroidery unlike the plain black scarves worn by most Saudi women. Her face veil was sheerer than commonly seen on the street. The outline of her face was easily visible behind the black voile.

Second daughter in her family, in which her older sister and oldest child in the family, was named after the Prophet's daughter, Amina did not feel as much the responsibility to be a role model for her younger siblings as older Sister Fatimah. Many first children often feel great responsibility for their younger siblings. Second-born Amina was playful and enjoyed a good joke even as she reverted immediately to acting like she was a religious devotee. She knew how to manipulate to get her way. She had tried this on Elizabeth after the first quiz in which she received the grade of 'C.'

Her response was, "I am only a weak woman. I must deserve a 'B.'" She stuck out a red pouty lip as she said this.

Elizabeth's response was the same she would have given an American student. "When you get 80% of the answers correct, you will receive a 'B.'" The pouty lip stayed stuck out on her classical Arabic face for several more minutes. Amina did not give evidence of the spirit of *En sha Allah,* 'if God wills it' in this situation.

~~~

Fairuz Maloof wore turquoise jewelry almost every day though she varied the colors of her blouses and dresses. It was almost like "turquoise" was a talisman in addition to being her first name. She had many different gold and turquoise pieces; earrings, necklaces, bracelets, hair barrettes and rings. She wore her wealth already and she was not even married. Apparently her family of doctors was rich enough to afford for this barely twenty-year-old to possess whatever she wanted.

Fairuz did seem to be compensating for the fact that she had been unable to pass the English test with high enough
~~~

grade to get into the female medical school program, instead enhancing her beauty and sexuality, though Elizabeth learned that any Saudi would tell you that sexuality was to be hidden and displayed only to one's husband.

Fairuz's father Dr. Maloof, was a prominent psychiatrist. Her oldest brother was an orthopedic doctor. The second oldest brother was a neurologist. The next was an ophthalmologist. And her fourth brother, just older than Fairuz was a pulmonologist resident. Her sister, who was two years younger, had married early though it was custom for her to wait until her older sister Fairuz was married first. However, Fairuz had met at least two possible suitors and rejected them. Her parents had found these men and arranged with their families for each of the man's parents to bring their eligible son to the villa to meet Fairuz's family and then Fairuz, the possible bride. In each case Fairuz had rejected them. After the second one was rejected, her parents gave in to the younger daughter who was pressing to marry her cousin whom she had not seen since she put on the *abaya* at age eleven. That marriage had already produced a son, so Fairuz was an aunt, but an old maid by Saudi marriage age averages.

Her parents were carefully screening women for the brothers. Her oldest brother, the orthopedic doctor, was already engaged.

Fairuz's English language test score was high enough to allow her to enter the nursing program but not the medical school. She accepted this as her lot in life, *En Sha Allah*, if God wills it.

Part of what Elizabeth discussed with these three students was what jewelry would be acceptable to wear with a nurse's uniform which for now was a simple white lab coat. She hoped that this was sufficient to educate Fairuz on what jewelry she would be allowed to wear when she really began to work. No dangling earrings that could catch on patient's hair or bedding.

Mouna, whose name means 'desire' or 'wish,' had been nicknamed 'Weesh' by her merchant father because she had been born while he was reviewing English language before going to India on a buying trip. He had originally learned English while he was enrolled as a child in the Riyadh International School. Because of his international travel as an importer/exporter, he valued languages and exposed his three children to English. Since her mother was also raised in a more international import/export household in Damascus, she too was somewhat conversant in English. Though Mouna could have passed the English exam and gone to the Women's Medical School, she instead chose the profession of nursing due to the influence of her *hajji* aunt who had visited Mecca for the *hajj*.

Her caring nature was evident in many ways as Elizabeth came to know Mouna. Despite blaming the driver probably falsely, for being late for class, Mouna was generous with her classmates. She shared her Arabic class notes since she knew her notes were better than theirs because she understood Elizabeth's English better. Elizabeth could see the students taking notes in Arabic in their notebooks on her English lectures. Mouna often arranged for study sessions before exams. During lab, she explained Arabic words that Elizabeth did not understand that came up during practice sessions. Mouna reached out to her classmates in friendship, inviting them to women's parties at her home. Eventually, she even invited Elizabeth and the other faculty to parties at her home. Mouna's mother being conversant in English was a wonderful hostess to them. Also, in Mouna's home, the females were more relaxed about covering their faces when a male entered a room full of women.

After a party where both students and faculty were in attendance, Mouna Shamoon explained that "Since my mother is from Syria where they are not so strict, she doesn't always remember to cover her face whenever men are around. So she doesn't make us do it either."

~~~

One day during class, Amina arose and said "Monthly blood" and went running from the classroom.

Though she wondered whether Amina was doing her usual manipulation, Elizabeth felt she must give her the benefit of the doubt so she said to the other students, "Let's take a break till she comes back. Fairuz, will you ask Nouri to bring us some tea?"

When Amina returned, she presented a hangdog look saying," Feel sick, need to go home." It appeared she had wiped off her red lipstick to give her face a pallor. Even her eyes looked more sunken. Elizabeth wondered if she had added *kole* eye shadow while wiping off her lipstick to make herself look sicker.

Since it was two-thirds through the class-time, Elizabeth decided they would just end early. "Let's drink our tea before you send for your driver, Amina. Something hot in your stomach will often help with menstrual cramps," she explained.

She went on, "We will make up this lost time next session."
~~~

She did not want them to think they could use this excuse to avoid their lessons. She made sure they understood the message. "We have to have all the hours required for this class, so if we have to stop early today, we will add an hour to another class later."

After putting their cups back on Nouri's tray, the three students trooped out and down the stairs with Amina looking entirely revived.

Chapter 12

Shemazzi Hospital

Amal made an appointment for Elizabeth to take the junior students to Shemazzi Hospital to visit the medical/surgical ward. This was part of their observational clinical laboratory. Shemazzi Hospital was a government hospital open to all patients, regardless of national origin or citizenship. There were several other hospitals in Riyadh that were available to only a certain population such as the National Guard Hospital or King Faisal Hospital. For a regular patient to receive services in these other special hospitals, it was necessary to be sent there by a doctor's request for admission.

Elizabeth met the three junior students in the National Saudia University for Girls nursing laboratory where she reviewed the regulations they needed to observe while in the surgical theater or the ward. They were wearing their new white laboratory jackets with their name badges from the university pinned to the lapels. The students adjusted Elizabeth's *abaya* and face veil for her as she still frequently had it come loose from simple movement. The young women never seemed to have this difficulty, probably because they had learned the skill of securing the various pieces of clothing and cloth as soon as they donned it after menstruation began, which is when most girls began to veil.

Amal, the secretary, called Mr. Rahman to ask for a car and driver to take them to Shemazzi Hospital. They waited for him just inside the wall of the front gate to the University where they could see the car with the university logo on the door when he drove up.

The students conversed in Arabic language as they stood together. Elizabeth listened as closely as she was able as she had begun to regularly study Arabic language both at night and morning in the flat. She had been able to get a textbook titled *A Course in Spoken Arabic* by Shafi Shaikh and another, *Modern Literary Arabic* by David Cowan at the bookstore on Airport Road. The Arabic language lessons promised in Houston Consulate had not yet started. Elizabeth felt she could not wait so she spent half an hour every morning studying the textbooks. But that did not provide listening skills she needed; consequently, she attempted to catch a few words or phrases whenever she had a chance to listen to others' conversations. Additionally, most of the television programs were in Arabic language, too, except for fifteen minutes of English news at night which were usually just reports of the King's daily activities. She even bought a *Koran* with Arabic script, transliteration and translation into English. She tried to follow the transliteration of the chants from the television.

This very morning, she had been reviewing in *A Course in Spoken Arabic,* the words for male relatives. She had just learned the word for brother – *akhu* and *amm* for uncle.

The students assumed she could not understand anything they said in Arabic. They knew that it was bad manners to be talking Arabic in front of someone who did not understand it. But Elizabeth knew it was to her benefit to be exposed to their conversation, so she did not admonish them. Instead, she slowly became more conversant without their being aware of it. When she heard Fairuz saying *akhu*-brother and *mustashfaa*-hospital, she was alerted. From listening carefully, she guessed that Fairuz was talking about her youngest brother whom she remembered was a pulmonologist resident at Shemazzi. Fairuz was informing her classmates that she would introduce them. Already Elizabeth knew this was forbidden for these Saudi girls. But Mouna's more liberal half-Syrian ways was apparently influencing them to break the Saudi sex segregation code.

When the car came, the three students piled into the back seat and Elizabeth took the front passenger seat. This was a different driver from any she had met before. Apparently he had been warned about interacting with females as he said nothing to them as he drove off. Elizabeth decided he must be Pakistani from the Paki suit he wore. She later learned they were called *shalwar kameez*.

She tried some English on him, "My name is Elizabeth Adams. I am from America. Where are you from?"

Indeed, the young man responded in the accented English of the Indian sub-continent, "I am from Yemen. I am Mr. Amari."

"How long have you worked for the university," she spoke slowly hoping he would not be too distracted from the fierce traffic they encountered as they neared the front of Shemazzi Hospital. The traffic was the usual jamming together of vehicles, each trying to threaten to nudge the others out of their way. A bus was parked just far enough away from the fifteen inch curb so that passengers would find it necessary to step down into the street before hiking their clothes in preparation to stepping up on to the high curb.

Mr. Amari skillfully wove his way close to the front walkway and said, "I have just started working for National Saudia University for Girls. What hour shall I come for you?"

Elizabeth answered, "Please come back and meet us here at exactly twelve o'clock." She knew the students would expect to go home to the big afternoon meal and rest time with their families. It would be necessary to get them back to the university for their family drivers to pick them up by 1:00 PM.She was already learning that time meant different things to different groups in Riyadh. This would give them almost three hours to observe in the hospital this morning.

She led the students to the front information desk and asked in English, "How do we get to the men's medical/ surgical ward?"

Seeing the confused look on the male receptionist face, Mouna spoke through her veil and translated Elizabeth's question into Arabic. The male receptionist's face cleared up as he explained with generous hand gestures, pointing toward the elevator. The three students followed Elizabeth like a flock of newly hatched blackbirds with their faces fully covered due to the hallway full of men.

When they exited the elevator on the second floor, Mouna again led by reading the Arabic labels on the not-too-clean wall, eventually guiding them in through a door where a nurse's desk sat against the wall of a long hallway. A male attendant exited a patient room near them.

Elizabeth said to him, "I am looking for Head Nurse

Najjar."

"She is with a patient in room number six," the man dressed in white slacks and shirt, replied in very understandable English, not even looking surprised to be addressed in English. His face was the taupe color of many Egyptians and his hair was a few shades of brown darker than his skin. "I'm an orderly. My name is Mustafa."

"How do you do, Mustafa? These are the nursing students from National Saudia University for Girls. I am their teacher Elizabeth Adams. Mrs. Najjar is expecting us, I think." Elizabeth did not offer her hand for a handshake as she might have done in California as she had learned of the Saudi revulsion for physical contact between non-related males and females even though Mustafa was probably not Saudi. Saudis seldom did this kind of attendant work. How this would work with female nurses taking care of male patients was still a puzzle to her.

"I will let Mrs. Najjar know that you are here," said Mustafa disappearing into room number six and reappearing followed by a mature, tan faced woman wearing a long white uniform and white veiled headdress, the kind Elizabeth associated with pictures of nurses in medieval hospitals.

"Mrs. Adams, the secretary, Amal, of the Nursing Department at National Saudia University for Girls told me your name," the woman said in clear but Egyptian accented English. Calling someone Mrs. even if they were not married was apparently a way of giving weight to their name Elizabeth was learning. "First, I will have Fareeda Seddik, our surgical nurse, take your girls on a tour of the hospital and surgical theaters, while you and I sit in my little office and plan the rest of your sessions here. I remember that Amal said you would like the students to come once per week for observation, yes?"

As they seated themselves by Mrs. Najjar s desk in a cubby-hole between two patient rooms, she continued her instruction to Fareeda. "Nurse Seddik, when you come back to the ward, let the girls take patient blood pressures."

As Elizabeth and Mrs. Najjar walked away, Nurse Fareeda began giving the students a lesson in how they should wear their face veil and *hijab*, hair scarf when treating male patients. Elizabeth could see Fareeda showing them just how much of their face could be visible.

Mrs. Najjar's cheerless cubby-hole office had one office chair behind the desk for her and a metal folding chair which leaned against the back wall. She unfolded the chair for Elizabeth. Other medical staff passed close behind Elizabeth's chair as they had their planning session.

"I believe that our secretary, Amal, told you that we are hoping to bring the students every Monday morning for their observational clinical. Is this still agreeable to you?" asked Elizabeth.

After assuring agreement for the schedule, the two women made a list of procedures that the students could safely perform with patients; blood pressures, temperatures, hydration levels, charting these measurements, assisting in bed bathes and feeding. Elizabeth promised to have the students properly instructed and prepared in these procedures.

Mrs. Najjar concluded the meeting by offering, "Would you like to have me give you a tour of the hospital, especially the office of medical director Dr. Awad?"

"Yes, I believe that it may be very helpful for me to meet the medical director. It will also be good for him to know who we are if he meets us in the hallway," agreed Elizabeth.

Nurse Najjar led Elizabeth to the administrative suite. As they walked she explained that Dr. Awad, the medical director, was a Saudi doctor trained in the United States. The first room they entered was a huge audience room with benches lining all the walls. Every spot was filled. Mrs. Najjar explained "Petitioners come and just wait for their turn to be called into see Dr. Awad. But we do not have to wait for that." She led Elizabeth across the huge room, avoiding other people sitting and waiting on the beautifully carpeted floor. Mrs. Najjar knocked vigorously on the door before opening it and gesturing to Elizabeth to follow her. The current petitioner to Dr. Awad, a short man in a dirty white *thobe*, just automatically stepped back when Mrs. Najjar entered.

"Dr. Awad, I want to introduce you to Nurse Adams, a new nursing instructor at the Nursing Department at National Saudia University for Girls." Mrs. Najjar slid her arm behind Elizabeth and pushed her toward Dr. Awad's huge wooden desk. Elizabeth did not stick out her hand remembering the Saudi prohibition between men and women touching. However, Dr. Awad stood and reached out his right hand thus breaking this 'no-touching' rule. His grip was strong. Though his English language was slightly accented, Elizabeth could distinguish his American English from the British English she so often heard here in Riyadh. Dr. Awad was tall compared to many Saudi men Elizabeth had seen in the streets. He spoke softly in Arabic to the dirty *thobed* petitioner who backed out of the office.

Dr. Awad gestured toward a round conference table behind his desk. The two women took chairs across the table from Dr. Awad.

"Well, Miss Adams, tell me about your training and previous work, please. I like to know about professional people who come into the hospital," said Dr. Awad.

Elizabeth gave a brief biography of her education and work life including her recruitment for this job by Dean Ashwari. She then went on to explain her goals for bringing her students here to Shemazzi Hospital.

"You are most welcome. We view our mission here is to provide both patient care and professional training for inhabitants of Riyadh and surrounding villages. I will always welcome you here in my office if you have requests." Dr. Awad signaled for a servant with a tea tray to place it on the conference table. The servant poured out a tiny cup of aromatic cardamom tea for each of them and then left the office.

Dr. Awad went on to inquire whether Elizabeth had a family. Learning that she was alone in the Kingdom, he inquired about whom she had met since she arrived. He seemed pleased when she told him of the Desert Ramblers and the trip to the desert to look for Saudi diamonds.

Having read the rules before she came to the Kingdom about Islam being the only religion that could be publicly practiced, Elizabeth was reluctant to discuss the Riyadh International Christian Fellowship. However, she did tell of the friendship with the other faculty, especially Jessie Edwards and Amy Burch.

Dr. Awad did not offer the usual two more cups of tea

excusing himself by explaining his need to continue his discussion with the previous supplicant. He went on, "This is not the Saudi way, to hurry with visitors but I am trying to finish all my work before leaving the Kingdom for a medical conference in Europe."

When Nurse Najjar and Elizabeth returned to the Medical/Surgical ward after a complete tour of the hospital including the basement full of old medical records and out of date or broken medical equipment, the students were dutifully following Nurse Fareeda Seddik from patient room to patient room. They took turns taking temperatures, blood pressure, etc. as Nurse Seddik felt they were too new to be allowed to do these fundamental measurements without immediate supervision. Elizabeth was glad to observe as well in order to determine whether there were any differences from what she had taught.

Chapter 13

Shemazzi Again

What Elizabeth had not seen while she was in Dr. Awad's office drinking cardamom tea, was that Fairuz had used the pay phone in the entry hallway to call the Pulmonary Ward to tell her brother Mahmoud, that she was in the Medical/Surgical Ward and that he should come and greet her. She had avoided telling him that her classmates were with her. She knew it was forbidden for him to see her classmates socially like this when they were with her professionally with their faces uncovered. But the students knew that this was the plan. There had always been ways to get around Saudi strictures about comingling of the sexes.

Her brother had left his duties temporarily and come upstairs to welcome his sister to the hospital. The pulmonary ward was in the basement so the climate and desert dust were better controlled and closer to the generator in case of emergency. He was not surprised to find her in the hallway with her classmates with their faces uncovered. Nurse Fareeda Seddik had left her charges for a few moments to go into the medication room in order to prepare some special medicine for one of the patients. Had she been there she would probably have prevented the conversation he had with unveiled Amina, getting her telephone number in order to arrange to meet in the canned vegetable aisle of the Jareer Street Grocery. He had immediately been transfixed by Amina's lovely face and demeanor. Though his parents were not pressuring him to marry right now, he realized that his sisters could not provide the kind of relationship he wanted with a woman. Marriage was the only approved way. He couldn't wait for his brothers to get married before him. He knew his parents were screening possible wives for his two other brothers and he did not relish the idea of waiting or of his parents choosing his wife for him. If he found his own sweetheart, he could somehow get his parents to invite her family to meet his family.

During the second Monday student visit to Shemazzi Hospital, after Amina and Mamoud had had their first clandestine meeting in the Jareer Street Market, they had arranged to sneak away from the others in the hospital. Mamoud on the telephone had described his car to her so she could find it in the hospital parking lot. She got into the back seat. Within a few minutes, he came out and got into the driver's seat and took Amina for a tour of the sections of the city near the hospital. Amina stayed in the back seat with her face covered. They looked like any Saudi family in the car with the husband driving and his wife in the backseat. None-the-less, they were able to communicate volumes.

Elizabeth had assisted Nurse Fareeda to find a more efficient way to organize the medicine room. It was not until she came out of that tiny room that Elizabeth discovered that Amina was not with her classmates. Fairuz made an excuse for her absence, saying, "Amina's cousin is a patient in the cancer ward. She went to visit him." Fairuz wanted to have Amina for a sister-in-law and so she told this lie to give her brother time alone with Amina. Elizabeth unquestioningly took Fairuz's explanation.

Elizabeth did not usually have direct contact with the male patients on this ward because her Arabic language was not sufficient though she continued her daily Arabic language studies. Also, she did not seem to be able to master the proper wrapping of her *hijab*, headscarf so that is did not unwind when she bent over a patient. She decided it was just better to let the students do the communicating with the patients.

On this second Monday visit to Shemazzi Hospital, Elizabeth had timed it so that she and the nursing students could follow the doctors on their daily medical rounds before leaving at noon. They always waited till the nurses were all done with patient bathes and bedding changes. At eleven when the doctors showed up, Amina was still not back on the ward. Elizabeth made a promise to herself to scold her soundly and even tell Amina she would have to do extra class work to make up for missing the Doctors' Rounds.

There were four doctors and two residents at this Rounds. Dr. Deng, a dark skinned Sudanese surgeon was the obvious lead doctor. He walked with a somewhat lofty attitude as he led his group into each patient room. All the rooms had at least two patient beds and all were occupied. He first asked the patients questions and then asked his residents what they thought. He seemed to have no regard for the fact that the other patients or their family in the room could hear everything said about the roommate. Dr. Awad brooked no conversation that was not directed toward diagnosis or whether such and such a treatment was working. Nurse Fareeda Seddik followed immediately behind him and stood at his side and slightly back as he questioned patients and doctors, ignoring the patient after the initial questioning except to order one of the residents to perform some procedure or specific examination. Nurse Fareeda carried a clipboard on which she wrote every instruction he gave either to the doctors or for the nurses. Her obsequious behavior to the doctors, especially to Dr. Deng was quite a revelation to Elizabeth, who was used to a more equal relationship with doctors in California. But she was distracted with worry by now about where Amina was and why she was not here with her classmates. She was so distracted that she did not recognize that one of the Saudi Arabian doctors, Dr. Fadel, was trying to flirt with her whenever they walked between patient rooms. He would sidle up beside her and ask questions such as "Where are you from? Did you come with your family?" which Elizabeth realized was his way of trying to find out if she was married.

As the group finished their Rounds, they milled around Nurse Najjar's desk with last minute doctors' orders. Dr. Fadel again brushed Elizabeth's arm supposedly accidentally as he whispered a request for her telephone number. She moved away from him as if she had not heard him. From her conversations with Jessie and Amy, she realized how dangerous it could be to allow any relationship with a Saudi man. Her colleagues had told stories of Western women being deported after relationships with Saudi men were exposed to their employers.

As they stood fully veiled, waiting for Mr. Amari in the partial shade of the entryway, Fairuz's brother, Dr. Mamoud Maloof, appeared. While the totally black veiled students would have been indistinguishable to most Westerners, the size, and height of the females and the distinguishing borders on *abayas* quickly helped friends or family identify a particular woman. Amina, being so slight and short, plus her almost transparent veil was easily recognized by Dr. Mamoud Maloof.

Fairuz distracted Elizabeth saying, "Mrs. Adams, come with me. Look at bulletin board in hallway?" Elizabeth followed her, completely missing Dr. Maloof passing a piece of paper to Amina. The announcement on the bulletin board was in English and Arabic describing an upcoming camel race. Elizabeth was innocently amused by this diversion by Fairuz and asked her, "Have you ever gone to a camel race?"

Fairuz attempted to keep Elizabeth in the hallway as long as possible so her brother and Amina could talk so she answered, "No, but my father and brothers like it."

"Are women allowed to go?" asked Elizabeth.

"Only sometimes in a separate section," answered Fairuz.

Elizabeth began to worry that Mr. Amari, the driver, might be waiting, so despite Fairuz attempting to slow her down with conversation, she returned to the entrance. Dr. Maloof had disappeared and the other students were getting into the backseat of the University car.

~~~

On the following Monday, the last hospital visit before *Hajj* would start, when the students would be away from campus, Elizabeth approached Nurse Najjar and Dr. Awad about allowing the nursing students to visit the Women's Medical/Surgical Ward as they so far, had only
~~~

observed on the Men's Ward. It seemed simply to have not occurred to either of them that the students should have this observational experience, too, perhaps because the students were scheduled for an observational visit to the maternity ward in their obstetrics class after *hajj*. However, the hospital was amenable to arranging for such a visit to the Women's Medical Surgical Ward. After one hour on the Men's Ward, they went to the small Women's Ward at the other end of the second floor. It was much smaller with half as many patient beds of the men's ward. It was two large rooms with eight beds in each. There was just one Egyptian female nurse and one female Yemeni aide. Neither spoke any English. After a discussion with the nurse, it was decided that Mouna would translate for Elizabeth and the female aide as she led them through each patient room and described their various afflictions and treatment plans.

In one room, they met an old woman with branded leg who had been a slave-nurse in one of the royal families. When Elizabeth saw the huge suppurating wound on her leg which left stains on the sheet, she inquired, "What happened? Was this an accident?" She realized that Bedouin women, cooking over open fires, had many accidents as demonstrated by the burned airplane on the runway.

Mouna translated Elizabeth's question for the elderly woman who replied, "I went to a traditional healer and she used a brand to treat the spot where I had frequent pain," or that is what Mouna said she said. The woman lifted her hospital gown to show a huge scar on her back and another on her hip. Mouna explained, "She said it has worked before."

Elizabeth tried to cover her own shock and disapproval

of this primitive medicine with only partial success. But the students, apparently being used to such attempts at pain control had already followed the nursing assistant to the next bed. However, Elizabeth was aware of the old woman watching her reaction with some amusement.

In the other big room, one of the beds was pushed into the corner and surrounded by an ancient rolling divider of scuffed white painted metal pipes with stretched dirty white cotton sheeting. The smell from behind this screen was detectable the moment the door opened. The students following Nurse Fareeda and Elizabeth recoiled at the smell. The patients in the other beds looked comatose or at least sleeping. Elizabeth wondered how they tolerated the smell. "What is the cause of the smell?" she asked Fareeda in a whisper.

"Septicemias," she replied. Then Fareeda lowered her voice so only Elizabeth could hear and said, "Self-induced abortion. Very bad! Rotten from inside. But we give her penicillin."

Chapter 19

Hajj for Infidels

As *hajj* approached, the Egyptian faculty and the Saudi administrative staff from the men's office began their preparations to leave Riyadh to go first to Medina and then to Mecca for the pilgrimage. A few days before the actual pilgrimage holiday was scheduled to start, they began to cancel their classes and disappear from campus. Patsy Elgin approached Elizabeth and Aisha, who was also new to the faculty, to ask them to sign her paper promising that if she did not come back at the end of Hajj, they would pay her two month salary in bond. Despite the story of what had happened to Ina's previous roommate, Patsy convinced them of her trustworthiness by giving them each an IOU in the amount of one month of her salary. Partly because Elizabeth was new here, she felt she should not refuse. Amy witnessed this transaction grimacing and gesturing to Elizabeth to no avail and later expressed her doubts because of what had happened to her and Jessie but the deed was done.

Amal, the Egyptian secretary, though a devout Muslim, had decided to avoid going to Mecca this year as she had done in the past. On the last day before pilgrimage was to start, when Amal, the secretary and Westerners were the only ones left in the Nursing Program at National Saudia

University for Girls, Elizabeth asked her "Why didn't you go?"

Amal from behind her typewriter explained, "The Prophet asked us to go only once in our lives. I went last year. Sleeping on a cot with people coughing nearby, uggg! I got sick, too." She made a sickly face to accompany her words.

"But the Nursing Department will be closed, yes? You don't have to come in to work, do you? The Dean told us Americans we had a vacation during *hajj*."

"Well I don't have to explain to the Dean that I am not going on the *hajj*," replied Amal. "No, I won't come in. The campus will be closed. Besides, Mrs. Edwards will not be here. They will call my mother while they are in Cairo." Amal always referred to the faculty by calling them "Mrs." and their last name. This was the first Elizabeth knew that Jessie and Amy would be away taking this opportunity to travel to Egypt during *hajj*. Apparently they had paid their two months bond out of their own pockets since none of the faculty was willing to sign their papers to pay the bond for them since Ina's former roommate had betrayed them by leaving them to pay her bond. That was why Amy had been so dismayed when she witnessed Elizabeth and Aisha signing Patsy's paper.

Elizabeth felt only a flicker of dismay at finding herself alone in this Arab city for two weeks. Perhaps she would take this opportunity to go to the U.S, consulate and register as an American citizen. Because Saudi Arabia was currently considered peaceful after getting over the 1979 invasion of the Grand Mosque during *hajj*, she had felt no need to rush to make herself known to the consulate when she first arrived.

The first morning of official *hajj*, the city was quiet. Busses were at a much reduced time schedule. Many of the foreign Muslim taxi drivers took this opportunity to do their lifetime duty of going on the *hajj*. Consequently there were fewer vehicles on the street. Even the occasional Bedouin riding down Airport Boulevard on his camel was not in evidence.

Elizabeth's shipment which included her autoharp, her portable typewriter and her electric sewing machine had arrived the week before *hajj*. She had loaded them into a taxi to bring them home from the customs office at the airport. Now she had all she needed to keep her busy in the flat. The souq was still open so she could shop for cloth to make some other long-sleeved, floor-length dresses. She would have time to tune the autoharp and learn some new songs from the folksong book she had included in her shipment.

Her flat-mate, Ina Brooks, had disappeared leaving only a note on the kitchen counter top notifying Elizabeth that she would be gone during *Hajj*. Ina was a curious woman, almost like a ghost seldom making her presence known but simply reminding Elizabeth in weird ways of her continuing residence. Ina kept her bedroom door closed and locked. This essentially deprived Elizabeth of access to the only external window in the flat. Elizabeth almost never even saw Ina in the Nursing Department at National Saudia University for Girls. Since Elizabeth had lived alone for so much of her adult life, she was glad to have the flat to herself and gave it no further thought.

Commerce did not cease during *hajj*. The *souqs* were perennially interesting to Elizabeth. The carpet *souq* was in a dim alley lined on either side with six yard by six yard shops which were stacked from floor to ceiling with all the rich variety of carpets from throughout the East and Middle East. Bedouin men from the desert stood in the middle of the alley with carpets spread before them, trying to sell them to the *souq* vendors. It reminded Elizabeth of the stories from her childhood about caravan routes, about the Casbah in spy movies and in *Lawrence of Arabia*. It was a seductive place.

The women's *souq* had booths of fabulous brocades, silks, velvets and some regular cotton prints which were more of Elizabeth's taste. Also, the cotton was more appropriate to the climate, Elizabeth thought. She purchased several lengths of cotton printed cloth. She had several dress patterns she had included in her shipment which were easy to adapt to the floor length dress requirement.

The other sundry requirements for sewing had their own booths as well; threads, braids, embroidered edging, lining, buttons, belt buckles, scissors, thimbles, zippers, sequins and Velcro. There was even a booth selling sewing machines, however Elizabeth was glad she had brought her own machine as she was familiar with it. Right at this point in her career, especially her career in Riyadh, she did not need the challenge of learning to use a newer model sewing machine. She had to learn too many new machines in the nursing department as it was.

And then there was the gold *souq* which was almost blinding in its brilliance. The necklace aprons of gold commonly given to the bride were secured to velvet backdrop walls behind the vendors. Belts made of gold medallion links were also secured to velvet display boards. There were horizontal bars filled with bangle bracelets. Glass cases in front held gold rings and earrings. The gold was more brilliant than similar pieces in California because almost all Saudi gold was 24 carat, though there were some pieces of 18 carat. Some of the gold pieces were faceted which caused them to seem even more brilliant. While Elizabeth was not tempted to purchase yet, she was bewitched by the shear magnificent glitter.

When she began to feel the walls close in on her from too much solitary endeavor in the flat, she would don her *hijab* and *abaya* and take to the streets to see who else had declined to go to the *hajj*. She tried covering her face with the double thickness of black cotton gauze, until she stumbled over a pile of construction gravel on the sidewalk. She decided it was safer to be recognized as a non-Saudi woman with her uncovered face than to fall flat on her face while trying to be faceless.

Jessie and Amy had arranged with their friend, Chuck Toiler, to pick up Elizabeth and drive her to the Riyadh International Christian Fellowship meetings which occurred during *Hajj*. She was glad of this diversion.

David Nelson, her guide for the Saudi diamond outing also took her for a drive in the dessert and to a nearby village which had been wrecked by the Muslim Brotherhood several decades before. Because it was the dry desert, the destruction of the mud houses was still visible in almost the same condition they had been left in forty-five years before. Elizabeth wore her *abaya, hijab* and black cotton gauze face cover until they had departed the city limits. She sat beside David in the front passenger seat of the army Jeep. They decided she could masquerade as his wife as *mutawahs* seldom bothered women who were completely covered.

David agreed to take her to the American consulate to register as an American citizen in Saudi Arabia. Besides the benefit of the American government's awareness of her presence in the Kingdom in case of civil unrest, the consulate also informed American citizens of important situations such as the following announcement which they reproduced in the regular newsletter for American citizens:

IMPORTANT NOTICE

In accordance with official orders and regulations currently in force, all expatriates coming to this country, whether muslims or non-muslims, are requested to abide by the regulations and customs of the country. It is, therefore, expressly forbidden for women to go out without covering their heads and limbs. Fines will be imposed on those breaking these regulations.

Thank you for your understanding and cooperation.

God's mercy and blessings be with you.

The university had neglected to inform the Western faculty of this new edict.

When they returned from that trip to the US Consulate, David invited her to spend the night in his villa inside the American Army consultants' compound. Most of the other residents, both families and single men had taken the opportunity of the *Hajj* to visit nearby countries. Elizabeth accepted his invitation, knowing she was breaking Saudi law for which she could be severely punished. But since her flat-mate was away, as were most other faculty, and the consultants' compound was empty, too, there seemed little risk anyone would discover this offense. There was not even the usual guard in the guard shack at the gate of the compound. Elizabeth did give a brief thought of her old boyfriend Graham Brown. But he was far away and David Nelson was here in Riyadh.

They had a lovely evening. David cooked spaghetti and meatballs. Elizabeth had not shared a meal alone with a man since she arrived in Riyadh. They watched a movie as David's villa was furnished with a video player. They both enjoyed the excitement of a new partner. David was well prepared with condoms which were not available, in fact forbidden in most pharmacies in this Islamic kingdom.

~~~

When the Believers returned from their pilgrimage to Medina and Mecca, they were almost to a person, sick with some kind of influenza which they had contracted while sleeping in close quarters on cots near other Muslim pilgrims from around the world. Elizabeth understood why Amal had declined a second visit to the pilgrimage sites. Within a week, the *hajjes* had spread their illness to the rest of the faculty and students. Classes were postponed until this epidemic had concluded.

Patsy Elgin did not return to the dismay of Elizabeth and Aisha, who had a family. With chagrin and some shame to be so taken in by a colleague, the two dug down and paid a month salary each. The Dean seemed smug as he accepted the Saudi currency, *riyals*. He declined to provide Patsy
~~~

Elgin's home address, or to undertake to get the University involved to find the absconder. His blatant disregard of the plight of the two fellow faculty members almost made Elizabeth want to give up and go home too. But she was no quitter and repeated to herself and to Aisha the so oft heard Arabic phrase *En Sha Allah* – If God wills it, that she would find this woman and get back their money.

The faculty discussed who of the remaining faculty could finish teaching the infectious disease unit. Elizabeth volunteered as her teaching load was so diminished compared to that in California.

Chapter 15

Dilemma

After the regular class schedule resumed, Amina, already in her *abaya* with her face veil thrown back over her head, lurked near the door as her *abaya* clad classmates started down the steps. After Elizabeth had gathered up her lecture notes and lesson plans, she became aware of Amina.

"Did you have a question for me, Amina?" she asked.

Amina slunk toward where Elizabeth was gathering up her things in preparation to going to her office. "Mrs. Adams," she started, and then burst into tears.

Elizabeth put her arm around her and drew her into a chair. "What is wrong, Amina, are you sick?" She realized now perhaps why the young woman had been so quiet and looked so pale during the last class.

"Mrs. Adams, please, I, I, I missed my monthly bleed." Amina hung her head and let the tears drop into her lap.

Immediately, the time missed by Amina in the Grand Rounds and the sidewalk appearance of Dr. Mamoud Maloof came to her mind. Elizabeth had known enough young girls in California who disappeared suddenly from class to often reappear a few days later looking pale.

Occasionally, other students in her California classes would gossip within Elizabeth's hearing about abortion or discussing herbal concoctions rumored to start one's period. If a person worked with young women, these situations were ubiquitous. But rather than put words in her mouth, Elizabeth waited quietly for Amina to explain her tears and fears.

Gradually, the tears ceased and Amina brought her reddened eyes up to meet Elizabeth's. "I think I have," long pause while she struggled to find the right word, "conceived a baby." She burst into tears again.

Elizabeth waited until Amina went on, "My father will kill me. I have brought shame to him. My name means 'faithful and trustworthy'." Her tears reappeared.

Calmly but with reproach, Elizabeth asked, "Why are you telling this to me? Who is the father of the baby? Isn't he the one to whom you should be telling this?"

After a time of calming herself in order to explain, Amina said, "Dr. Mamoud Maloof is the father but his family will not have me if I am spoiled. And he go off to England to have another residency. He tell me 'Get rid of it'."

"Amina, I expect you think I can help you get rid of this fetus, but I am not an abortionist. And I do not know anyone here who performs such surgeries. I believe it is illegal to do abortions in Saudi Arabia. Did Dr. Maloof offer to do it?"

Amina burst into tears again. Elizabeth remembered the times that Amina had tried to manipulate her by asking to stop class for prayer time and pleading for an undeserved grade. None-the-less, her predicament now seemed authentic. However, Elizabeth was still new enough to Saudi Arabia to not be completely aware of the danger to Amina's life from the males in her own family who would see this as shaming their honor. They would see it as an abdication of their own providing for their family's honor. The government would not see it as a crime if they killed her to protect the family honor.

Being unable to think of other options at the moment, Elizabeth said, "Let me think about this. I will meet you out by the fountain tomorrow an hour before class and we can discuss what to do. Can you stand to wait till then?"

Amina looked hopefully up at her, wiping her tears on her black face cloth as she donned her *abaya*. Before exiting the classroom, she turned and gave Elizabeth a quick hug, saying, "*En Sha Allah*," If God wills it.

On the bus going back to the flat with Amy and Jessie, Elizabeth was tempted to ask their advice, but for some reason which she did not understand herself, she did not. But she felt the need to talk to somebody about Amina's situation before she met her tomorrow.

She seldom used the telephone in the flat as she felt sure that the line was tapped. The few times she had used it, she heard the clicks that she had been told were clues that someone was listening. Nonetheless, she took the chance and called David Nelson. When they had last been together, they had decided upon some code words that could be used on the telephone. If she needed to talk to him, she should say, "I heard from your mother. She says meet her in Jareer Street." That would mean Elizabeth wanted David to meet her. They had agreed that the *falafel* shop was a good place to meet. Then David would say, "Tell my mother to come at four," to let her know what time to meet. The Saudis would respect a meeting between mothers and sons, they decided, and since most Arabs understanding of English on the telephone would be rudimentary, the nuances of using these codes should elude them.

They arranged to meet that afternoon after prayer time. Somehow, Elizabeth felt free to tell David Nelson of Amina's predicament and how she felt somewhat responsible since the girl had been under her supervision at the time she would have committed this crime, for indeed, it was a crime in Saudi Arabia.

David informed her of the cases he had heard in which fathers and brothers had indeed assassinated their daughters and sisters to protect the family honor. These cases never made it into English media such as *Al Arabia*, the Saudi newspaper or the evening news. These stories were known here in the Western community only through word of mouth. David had heard them from Jordanian friends who were more liberal in their thinking than the Saudi soldiers he trained. David did inform her that the girl Amina was indeed in jeopardy for her life. Only last week, a friend of David's had described a women being stoned in the dead-end street under his villa's second story window. The man who told this story had heard the roar of a mob and went out on his tiled rooftop balcony to check for the source. Several cars had pulled up blocking the dead-end street near the *wadi*. He saw an *abaya* clad woman with feet and hands bound, and a black cloth bag over her head dragged from the backseat of a car and thrown to the ground. Prayers were chanted before the crowd; both men and women began to hurl stones until there was no noise or movement from their target. There were no police.

When the crowd ran out of energy to throw stones and it seemed they felt confident the woman was dead, several men, presumable family members, dragged the body out from under the stones, wrapped the whole thing, covered head and all in a white sheet and tucked it in the back of a van. Some of the participants walked away. Other got back into their cars and drove away. Nobody bothered to scatter the remaining stones.

David went on to tell Elizabeth of the other stories of family justice he had heard. Then he said, "Have you heard of the movie 'Death of a Princess?' It's illegal to bring that video into the Kingdom, but there is a guy in our compound who smuggled one in. Shall I borrow it so we can watch it?"

They began to discuss options for Amina to avoid death by family justice; abortion, a quickie wedding, smuggling her out of the kingdom. Abortion was illegal in the Kingdom. A quickie wedding – say 'shotgun wedding' in the West – was almost never an option here as the family honor was already damaged. David promised to ask around among the US Army consultants about abortionists as well as to borrow the "Death of a Princess" video. But this would not give Elizabeth any specifics to share with Amina when she met her at the fountain in the morning.

Making an excuse to Amy and Jessie about needing extra class preparation time, Elizabeth went to the office early to review her nursing obstetrics textbook on what chemicals and foods to avoid during pregnancy and what their side effects might be. The old wives' tale of the malaria drug, quinine, being an abortifacient had no modern research; however, quinine was to be avoided during the first trimester. Hum, maybe it did work. Since malaria was still an occasional affliction of people coming to this desert city, people who had caught it in more moist places, it was available in pharmacies. Most pharmacies did not require a prescription for easily available treatments.

The other old wives' tale she remembered hearing about was hot bathes. It was not in the obstetrics textbook, except as a warning to pregnant women to avoid soaking too long. These were the only two ideas she could suggest to Amina.

There was no other faculty or students in the compound near the fountain. Elizabeth removed her *abaya* and sat on the edge of the pool surrounding the fountain. She sat facing the wall that protected the courtyard from eyes in the street so she could see Amina. She had not to wait long. The veil camouflaged Amina's suffering until she removed it revealing a puffy face and red-ringed eyes. Elizabeth patted the edge of the pool showing Amina where to sit close to her so they could talk without risk of eavesdroppers.

"How are you, my dear?" Elizabeth asked.

Amina's face crumbled almost into tears again but she struggled to keep control here in this 'only for women' courtyard but the struggle was visible to Elizabeth. "Help me, Mrs. Adams," was her only reply. It was obvious that she was very close to breaking down.

After the stories David had told her the evening before, Elizabeth realized how important this situation was for Amina. Her life was in jeopardy if she did not get rid of her pregnancy. This was more than just shame for the family. It meant excising the family shame by erasing Amina. Of course, there was always the possibility that her period was just late and she was not pregnant, as it sometimes was in young women, but it was unlikely since Amina had confessed to having intercourse with Dr. Mamoud Maloof.

Elizabeth explained, "The only things I have thought of to try to bring on your menses are these. Some people say that taking quinine, the malaria drug, helps cause a spontaneous abortion. This is not well researched, but it is worth a try. And the other thing that could work is soaking in a tub of hot water. That involves raising your body temperature like making your body seem like its sick. You could try these first. If they don't work, we can look for other solutions."

Even these simple remedies cheered Amina up. "I try quinine now," Amina said. "Could I drink quinine water? I see it in store." She pointed to the store across the street from the campus gate.

"Well, you could start with that, but the malaria medicine from the pharmacy is more powerful," said Elizabeth.

As she taught her following class, she was aware of the momentousness of this conversation and how it could affect the life of one of her students. Amina seemed more attentive than she had at the last session as she seemed to feel she might have some hope of coming out of this alive.

Chapter 16

"Death of a Princess"

By Wednesday evening, which was like Friday evening in the USA, David Nelson had been able to borrow the video of "Death of a Princess." Because it was against Saudi law to import this particular video, this smuggled version was in high demand among Westerners. David picked up Elizabeth after prayer time. He had purchased frozen pizza and popcorn so they would not have to go to one of the fancy hotels which was the only place a couple like themselves could feel safe eating together in public. *Mutawahs* avoided the big hotels.

David had a friend who worked for the United Nations who had a flat in a regular commercial block of flats, not one run by any organization such as David's which was run by the Saudi National Guard. Consequently, there was no 'watch-dog' at the door to observe who and what went in and out of peoples' flats. That friend felt free enough to make his own wine in his bathroom. Occasionally David's friend Kenneth shared this forbidden drink with friends. David had purchased a bottle from him to accompany the pizza. David also had a little liquor shelf in the cupboard beside the refrigerator because occasionally, liquor was shipped in for the American consultants under the label of 'Furniture.' David seldom drank except on special occasions such as this. Red homemade wine went well with the pizza. It reminded Elizabeth of home.

The first thing they did after arriving in David's villa was to heat up the oven and pop in the pizza. David had already set up the video. Then he poured some of Kenneth's wine which came in a reused glass grape juice bottle. They sat together on the sofa and tasted the wine while waiting for the pizza. The wine was still a little raw but since neither had tasted any recently, they enjoyed it. Elizabeth shared the conversation she had with Amina. As soon as the pizza was ready, David started the video which turned out to be grainy since it had been copied off a copy from a television in England. But it was still understandable and compelling. A British journalist tried to find the truth of a story going around Middle Eastern literati that a Saudi princess and her lover have been executed for their crime of love. He got a number of different versions of the story. It felt especially urgent since Elizabeth had just given advice to her student Amina, about how to avoid a similar fate.

The content of the video was almost discouraging enough to counteract the effects of the wine, but Elizabeth and David felt safe enough in the US Army Consultants' compound protected by the Saudi National Guard so that eventually, their inhibitions were overcome and they enjoyed the pleasures of sex. They waited a while afterward and brushed their teeth before attempting to leave. Elizabeth used a new toothbrush provided by David. They needed to wait to make sure there was no alcohol on his breath and that he would not be accused of drunk driving or that neither of them could smell of outlawed alcohol before taking Elizabeth back to the University flats.

When classes resumed the following week, Amina,

though less pale and having less red rimmed eyes, again stayed after class to report on the failure of the methods Elizabeth had suggested she try.

"Nothing, nothing, and nothing!" she said as soon as the other students were out of hearing distance. She clutched and squeezed her hands in front of her abdomen as if that might cause a miscarriage. "What should I do? Is there anything else?" She was certainly unlike the manipulative, playful girl Elizabeth had experienced during the first part of the semester.

"You have all those older women in your house, your mother, your aunt, your father's mother. I guess they can't help you now," remarked Elizabeth, hopeful that Amina might negate this statement.

It seemed only to unleash the tears again. "They would think I should be punished to keep the family honor just like my brothers and father."

What to do, what to suggest now? She certainly did not want Amina to end up like the princess in the video. Elizabeth wondered if Dr. Clough at King Faisel Hospital might suggest other possibilities, or know stories of how others had solved similar situations to avoid tragedy. On the other hand, telling anyone else, especially a doctor in the Royal Hospital who could be close to the Royal Family, could jeopardize Amina more. Elizabeth was unaware because of her newness in the Kingdom of how the Royal Family did pretty much whatever they wanted, ignoring the *mutawahs*, the fundamentalist religious police whenever possible. It was hard, being the only medical professional to know this student's dilemma. There was some relief in sharing her concerns with David Nelson, but he had no solutions to offer. Or did he?

They had decided that making dates in advance rather than using the telephone was a safer way to keep their meetings private. Jessie and Amy knew she was seeing the man she had met at the Desert Ramblers and that she sometimes went with him instead of attending the Riyadh International Christian fellowship with them, but they were not aware of the intimacy Elizabeth and David were now sharing. And if they found out about Amina's situation, they would certainly blame Elizabeth as it had started under her supposed supervision of the students while in the hospital.

After the next class, without prompt, Amina waited, acting like she was taking extra time with her *hijab* and *abaya* until her classmates had departed before looking beseechingly at Elizabeth, "They will kill me if they find out. I think Mother has been checking my waste basket for bloody napkins. What should I do?"

Having no new ideas to offer, Elizabeth asked, "Your classmates, Mouna and Fairuz, could they help?" Elizabeth was thinking her peers might be the most sympathetic to her situation especially since the father was the brother of Fairuz.

"Oh, no, no! Fairuz cannot know. If she told her family, there would be no hope for me and he would be in trouble, too." Amina was emphatic in her posture and movements as she said this.

Elizabeth wondered why Amina cared what happened to him since he was abandoning her, nonetheless, Elizabeth decided to explore why Dr. Mamoud Maloof was not taking responsibility. "Why don't the two of you just run away to Bahrain and get married?" Elizabeth had already heard that Bahrain was the playground for Saudis trying to avoid their own religiously repressive regime. They could have an Islamic wedding there and let their families sort it out later, she thought. But she was still too new here to understand all the implications.

"He already gone! He finishing residency in London. I think he like marry me when he get back. But not if I have baby already, even if it's his. Too much shame!" She dropped her *abaya* clad head and shoulders almost as if she agreed. Then she went on, "I'm supposed to marry my cousin Najib. He been waiting for me since we were children."

This was indeed a dilemma. For that Elizabeth could think of no solutions. However she wanted to give this young woman some hope.

"What about Mouna? She seems a sympathetic friend. Also, I think her family is more accepting of modern ways. Could you tell her?" Elizabeth asked.

Uncertainty covered Amina's face as she considered this possibility.

Meanwhile, Elizabeth did not want Amina doing any damage to herself by trying to abort the fetus by mechanical means. She had seen a few women, even in California where abortions were legal, come into the medical surgical ward suffering from internal infections from having shoved some instrument up into their uterus attempting to end a pregnancy.

"Promise me that you will not try to kill this baby by

sticking something up in you, OK?" she said to Amina.

She could see from the slow calculating response that crossed the girl's face, that this thought had not occurred to Amina before. Fearful that she might have put a dangerous idea in Amina's head, Elizabeth put both hands on Amina's shoulders and drew her around to face where Elizabeth sat in the chair. Amina was so small that they were almost eye to eye, despite the fact that Elizabeth was sitting. "Do NOT try putting anything up inside you. It will not work. It will make you sick. It could kill you. Promise me!"

Slowly, tentatively, Amina looked Elizabeth in the eye. "Oh I will not. Maybe I can talk to Mouna. Maybe." She began to gather up her things.

Elizabeth watched Amina as she departed wondering if that calculating look meant she might go home and try to stick some sharp object up into her uterus, never mind her warning.

Chapter 17

Solutions?

In planning for the spring semester, Elizabeth decided the junior students needed a more modern updated nursing experience than she thought they could receive at Shemazzi Hospital. Besides, Dr. Fadel had become quite annoying with his attempts to touch her when she and the students went on Rounds. Elizabeth hoped Amina would still be able to be there to accompany them on clinicals next semester. After discussing the nursing clinical situation with Jessie and Amy, they suggested she contact a Scottish nurse, Jenny McFarlane, who worked at the National Guard Hospital. Amal made an appointment for her and ordered the driver, Mr. Amari.

Arriving at the very modern courtyard of the National Guard Hospital, she asked Mr. Amari, the driver, to return in an hour. Elizabeth hated asking him to wait in the sun. Even though it was the end of November, sitting in an automobile in the desert sun then, was still too dangerously hot. He could drive around in the air-conditioned car for an hour since it was unlikely there was a shady spot nearby. The university did not seem to mind how much gasoline they used up since it was pumping out of the ground here every day.

The front reception desk of the National Guard Hospital was every bit as modern as any hospital in Los Angeles. As in Shemazzi Hospital, the receptionist was a handsome young man. He called up to the medical surgical unit and asked them to send someone down to accompany Mrs. Elizabeth Adams.

Jenny McFarlane, a tall slender redhead, greeted her when she arrived and ushered her in to a table in the back of the nurses' station. Elizabeth found her Scottish burr so attractive. Jenny ordered a tray of tea from a young man who seemed to be standing by waiting for orders. It appeared very quickly and he set it on the round table between them. Meanwhile, Elizabeth explained what she hoped for her students during the next semester.

"Surrrrrre an we can prrrovide that," she assured Elizabeth.

As the women talked and drank their cardamom tea from the tiny china cups, Elizabeth felt comradely warmth from the Scottish nurse. She asked if she could have a tour of the medical surgical unit in order to properly prepare the students. As they walked through the patient rooms, Jenny gave the diagnoses and treatments of each patient without even referring to notes or measurement clipboards hanging on the end of each bed. One such diagnosis, "infection from female genital mutilation" was something Elizabeth vowed to discuss later with her.

While the women patients who were from families of the National Guard soldiers were on the unit, they were separated at the far end of the hallway with a divider so that patients well enough to get up and walk around or any women visitors would have a place to be unveiled as they visited their female family members.

"I am just aboooouut to finish my shift. Would you like to go to the hospital cafeterrrrria and get a coffee or bun?" asked Jenny.

"Oh, yes, that would be good. I have time. But let me go to the front door and tell Mr. Amari the driver as he won't have to wait for me for an hour," replied Elizabeth.

The two nurses enjoyed American coffee which was a rarity in Riyadh outside of fancy hotels. Jenny inquired about the students and the nursing school as she had never had clinical students before. Elizabeth asked about the female genital mutilation patient.

Jenny said, "There is an elderly woman in the old town near the Murrabah Palace who does clitorectomies, infibulations and cutting of labias. This is not the first one of her patients we've had in here." All Jenny's "r"s were a burr.

"Is that legal here?" asked Elizabeth.

"No, it's not legal but it's not the sort of tradition that families want to give up and also who would you report it to? Not the *mutawahs*, nobody gets punished for carrying on this tradition. I've seen several cases worse than this one," replied Jenny.

As they talked, Elizabeth felt safe to tell her that one of her students was pregnant outside of marriage and in jeopardy of fatal punishment.

"Do you have any suggestions for how to keep my student safe?" she concluded.

"Oh, that's a danger. We have had a woman or two here that needed treatment after a botched back street abortion.

I'm trying to remember what I heard about it at the time. Let me ask the man who cleans for us. He seemed to know everything about underground activities in Riyadh."

"Well, I guess there is still time. I think she probably got pregnant right before *hajj*," said Elizabeth. She must be about nine weeks pregnant right now. If she's going to get an abortion, it shouldn't wait too long."

The women agreed to meet the following Thursday in the Jareer Street Bookstore. There were always plenty of foreigners there. They would attract no suspicion and then they could take a cab to the Riyadh Palace Hotel and order some Saudi Champagne which was a pitcher of cut-up fruit marinated in Seven-Up. If they tried to enter the hotel each woman alone, they would be viewed with suspicion, but if two women arrived together in the cab, it was assumed they were each other's chaperon and not up to some nefarious sexual adventure.

~~~

Meanwhile, whenever her mind was not otherwise occupied, Elizabeth cast about for other solutions. Every Western person she came into contact with might have a possible solution. She felt desperate enough to risk discussing it as she had come to feel almost like Amina's situation was her own.

She questioned David, "Is there any way we could spirit my student out to another country where abortion is safer and more available?"

He responded, "I've heard there is another guy in our compound who has bought false documents from this Egyptian forger. Bahrain is a pretty open place where
~~~

Saudis go to have fun. I bet there is an abortionist in Manama, the capital."

"But how would we smuggle her out? Even if your Arabic was perfect, and you could act as her guardian, her *sohbah*, a Saudi girl would be on her father's passport. Even if she were veiled, they would be suspicious at the passport control at the airport." Though she said it to David, it was almost as if she were discussing it with herself. But he agreed that a foreigner taking a veiled Saudi girl out of the country was almost impossible unless he rented a camel and rode toward the Jordan border.

Next, Elizabeth decided to approach Mrs. Shaker the woman from the Riyadh International Christian Fellowship who was involved in the women's prison ministry. Elizabeth guessed that anyone involved in such work would know of people who helped imprisoned women solve difficult problems.

She remembered from the previous Friday worship service that Rev. Davis had announced that the drama group was starting a new Christmas play and that Mrs. Shaker was in charge. Elizabeth got her telephone number from Jessie Edwards who warned her again about the hazards of getting involved with Mrs. Shaker. Elizabeth tucked the reminder back in her mind behind the urgent need to help Amina. She called Mrs. Shaker and inquired, "Do you need any women readers for the parts in the play?" She did not want to discuss Amina's situation on the telephone as she had heard they were all tapped in the office as well as in the block of hospital worker flats.

Mrs. Shaker couldn't have been more excited or welcoming, "Oh, yes, this play 'The Christmas Dinner' by

Thomas Wilder has six female parts. It is always hard here to get enough women to fill all the parts. Oh, yes, please, join us. I'll ask Chuck Toiler to pick you up as he knows how to get to where we are meeting here at the minister's villa. He likes to read a man's part usually. We'd love to have you. We hope to have it ready for Christmas because there are so few things allowed here at Christmas. A Christmas play gives us Christians a little feeling of celebration, too, even though we have to keep it secret. I'm sure you know such things are forbidden by the Saudis."

Elizabeth did wonder at this convoluted thinking of the Christians in Riyadh, that it was OK to deceive as long as it was for a Christian purpose. But she remembered the rule that had been in her contract, to promote nothing non-Islamic in the Kingdom. She had given such injunctions little thought before she had arrived in Riyadh.

Chuck picked her up as planned and drove her to a compound with several nice villas around a common courtyard. Several cars were already parked in the courtyard. Mildred Davis, the minister's wife ushered them into the front parlor where the play reading was to be held. It was much more extravagant than most Christian ministers at home, Elizabeth thought. Later she learned that this was the compound of a Saudi prince under whose protection the minister and his wife lived.

Mrs. Shaker quickly distributed the mimeographed copies of "The Christmas Dinner" and parts for the different characters. After the first 'read through,' Mrs. Davis invited the players to come across the hall to a table spread with western cookies and Middle Eastern treats such a *baba-ganoush*, which is a roasted egg plant dip, *hummus,* ground chickpeas and toasted bagel chips.

Elizabeth took this opportunity to follow Mrs. Shaker into the hallway and when they were alone, she described Amina's dilemma. She discovered that Mrs. Shaker and Mrs. Davis, the minister's wife were in cahoots in the women's prison work. "Please, Elizabeth, let me tell Mrs. Davis about your problem. She always has good ideas," said Mrs. Shaker sotto voiced. They waylaid Mrs. Davis by following her toward the kitchen as she went to replenish a pitcher of juice. Her kitchen was very modern, much more splendid than the utilitarian kitchen in the hospital flats. Elizabeth noticed that it had one of the new microwave appliances.

Elizabeth repeated the dilemma of Amina and her own feeling of responsibility because it happened under her supposed supervision in the hospital.

Despite being the minister's wife, or perhaps because of being the minister's wife, Mrs. Davis, like Mrs. Shaker, did not seem shocked.

"Oh my dear, your student is in great danger," she responded. "I have gone to the American consulate to help a US citizen to break her contract and go home for an abortion, but a Saudi girl, well that's much different. What thoughts do you have?" inquired Mrs. Davis turning to Mrs. Shaker.

Elizabeth was relieved that these very Christian women were not shocked at the idea of abortion as she knew that some Christian women she had met at home in California were often strongly opposed.

Mrs. Shaker went on with another crushing story, "There was a Filipina girl who worked as a nanny in a Saudi home. She was regularly raped by the master of the house during his wife's pregnancy, with the wife's consent and connivance. The girl had no days off to be able to seek outside help. She was essentially a prisoner in the villa. When the girl eventually got pregnant, the wife accused her of stealing silverware and she was put into the Riyadh Women's Prison. That's where I met her. The prison is so dreadful with forty women imprisoned in a thirty by thirty foot space with only one floor toilet and one water faucet a foot off the cement floor. No furniture! But the girl was able to connect with some other wrongly imprisoned women who suggested remedies. We were able through friends who visited them to provide her with the herbs she asked for and she had a spontaneous abortion in prison. Then the Saudi family decided to drop the charges of stealing and wanted her back. Poor girl! We helped her through the Philippines Consulate to break her contract and go home. She lost all her pay, of course."

This was Elizabeth's first brush with the dreadful conditions often suffered by Asian women employed in Saudi households. Since arriving, the only Filipina women she had met were a few nurses in Shemazzi Hospital. But her encounters with them had only been about patient issues. Korean women nurses also served in their government's labor program where there were labor contracts between the countries. These nurses lived in the hostel run by the hospital. The hostel was locked most of the time. They were bussed to and from the hospital and allowed only a day off every other week. The contrast between treatment of Western nurses and the Koreans and Filipinas shocked Elizabeth.

Mrs. Davis and Mrs. Shaker assured Elizabeth that

they would give this situation their best thinking and consideration.

Chapter 18

Jareer Street

In her usual pragmatic and systematic nurse way, Elizabeth made a chart of pros and cons, possibles and impossibles about how to approach finding a non-lethal solution to Amina's problem.

Abortion abroad	Abortion in Riyadh	Abortifacient	Carry to term
Need passport for a male guardian and for Amina. Have to pay lots of money to find an abortionist	*May be easier but more dangerous. More likely to be caught*	*Unpredictable outcome but less dangerous unless she becomes toxic*	*Shame & Assassination by family*

Almost all Westerners were horrified by the Saudi tradition of male family members killing a sister or daughter for unmarried sex.

Elizabeth decided she needed to know exactly what the *Koran* prescribed for 'fallen women' so she took the bus to the Jareer Street Bookstore. The *Koran* section of the bookstore was amply supplied with Arabic versions, Urdu versions, and any number of English translations. She finally chose the translation by Abdallah Yousef Ali, an Egyptian. This version had a small English language summary of each section in the table of contents. The English was side-by-side with the Arabic on each page of *surahs,* verses. Additionally, this one had a red silk binding with gold imprinted decoration. This version appeared like the ones she had seen positioned on a carved stand in front of apparent religious scholars as they sat on the ground or sidewalk in the shade of a wall. She had heard that the *Koran* must never touch the ground which was why they required a stand, she supposed.

She intended to read the book from front to back however, in the interest of speed; she started by reading just the specific *surahs* which dealt with fornication or adultery. The only reference to punishment for such behavior she could find was for the offender to receive lashes.

By now, she had heard enough reports of women being stoned to death as well as viewing the "Death of a Princess" documentary that she realized such punishment did indeed happen and must be of tribal origin rather than religious. Regardless of the impetus, the woman got killed.

Elizabeth felt she needed a sympathetic person to bounce her thoughts off, so she called David Nelson. They agreed to meet after the Sunday evening Desert Ramblers meeting and decide then where they could go to talk. Saudis often ate dinner late, perhaps at 8 PM and then gathered socially afterward so David and Elizabeth would not seem unusual to be out driving around that late in the evening.

Elizabeth brought her chart of possibilities to share with David to get his ideas on what might be the best choice. She had come to trust him even in this short time. Besides, they were both guilty of the same crime as Amina. She realized whatever path they thought best they would have to persuade Amina to cooperate. The chart felt like it was burning a hole in her jacket as she listened to a lecture on species of desert lizards.

When they went out, the Street was full of life at 10 o'clock in the evening. She walked with David to where he had parked his car beside one of the fourteen inch high curbs which were common on most main streets. He had to pull out from the curb slightly so she could open the door to get into the backseat. He drove to his own Army Consultants Compound. There was no one in the guard shack. No need to lie!

Inside his villa, David offered Elizabeth a glass of whiskey from the latest 'Furniture' shipment the Army had received. She declined, knowing that she would be teaching the following morning. Besides, she wanted to stay clear-headed for this conversation and David would not have alcohol on his breath during the ride home. So they drank chilled pineapple juice.

She showed him the small chart of possible solutions and waited for a response.

David answered with a question, "As a nurse, have you had anything to do with abortifacients? What are they?"

Elizabeth explained what she had found in the history chapter of her obstetrics nursing textbook. "It mentioned a few of the common ones from ages past but did not tell how to concoct them. It listed artemisia, tansy, penny royal, and even catnip. I remember seeing a medicinal herb book at Jareer Street Bookstore. I need to go take a look and see if any of these are described in there."

"I'll pick you up tomorrow evening after prayer time and

we can go take a look. But now, could I persuade you to come into my lair? I still have rubbers so we don't have to rely on eating weeds," he said with a laugh as he slid his arms around her.

He was as good as his word. They arrived at the bookstore next evening just as it reopened after the fourth prayer time of the day. Jareer Street Bookstore was usually a safe place for couples who were not married to each other to go safely together. Nonetheless, inside the store they separated and each went to their own section until they confirmed that there were no men who looked like officers of the Committee for the Promotion of Virtue and the Prevention of Vice inside the store. Elizabeth found an *Encyclopedia of Herbs and their Uses.*

"I found all four of those herbs in this encyclopedia so I think I'll buy it but the ways to prepare the concoctions are not specific enough. I want to go to the men's university library to see if the medical section has anything. I already checked in the women's library and there are hardly any medical books there. The men's library has only a few hours per week when women students and faculty are allowed in as it's forbidden to the male students and faculty during those hours," Elizabeth explained.

Not finding anything in the Men's Library except modern medical textbooks during her Wednesday morning's two hour session, Elizabeth realized she would need to try to find the herbs mentioned either growing or sold here in the city and then she would need to experiment. She remembered the flower bed near the front of the administration building. The photos of plants in the *Encyclopedia of Herbs and their Uses* would have to suffice as she tried to identify the plants.

Artemisia, sometimes called the 'peacock flower' was often very tall, not likely to grow in desert gardens. Apparently African slaves had used it to keep from providing slave children for their masters.

Tansy looked to be easy to grow, in either full sun or some shade. The herb book listed a number of uses for treating worms in children, for epileptic seizures, fevers, gout but nothing about being an abortifacient. However, it did warn pregnant and nursing mothers not to ingest it which confirmed for Elizabeth its historic uses. If you could give it to children, it couldn't be that toxic, she surmised. However, it did say "it induces venous congestion of the abdominal organs." That should cause contractions.

Pennyroyal, like tansy could be used to repel fleas and mosquitoes. However, it could cause liver damage, kidney damage, massive multiple organ failure, excessive bleeding, and death. That did not sound like a good option and besides; Elizabeth had not seen any possibility of it being grown in the desert.

Catnip tea was reported to stimulate uterine contractions, which could help women or girls get their periods. Amina was already too late for that. It could also promote excretion of the placenta after childbirth. This sounded like a possibility, but Elizabeth had never seen catnip growing and it did not seem like a desert plant. Of course, people could grow it in pots, but where would a person buy seeds here. She had never seen a seed rack like she remembered in California garden shops.

She wished she could consult with some other medical people here but she felt they certainly would not want to be associated with any such project. And the more people she talked with about it, the more she put herself in jeopardy for being found to break Saudi laws. Also, she needed to know the dosage for how much tansy should be effective.

~~~

The schedule in the Saudi university semester system meant that Western Christian faculty members would normally have been expected to work on Christmas Day except this year it came on Thursday which was a day off anyway. This was fortunate as the Western faculty was reluctant to ask for their holiday off due to the injunctions about "promoting nothing non-Islamic."

Jenny and Amy hosted a small Christmas party in their flat on Christmas afternoon. They had no Christmas tree but instead had used their full length mirror and taped glittery objects from the souq in the shape of a tree as decorations. Homemade cookies reminded guests of Christmas at home. They invited all the National Saudia University for Girls nursing faculty, a few friends from the English Department and a few from the Riyadh International Christian Fellowship. Elizabeth persuaded Jessie Edwards to invite Jenny McFarlane. Jessie sent Chuck Toiler to pick her up at the National Guard Hospital nurses' residence for the party.

The Riyadh International Christian Fellowship scheduled "The Christmas Dinner" performance on Friday afternoon December 26th. They had been having practice sessions after church service on Fridays and one evening during the each workweek. During these sessions as well as at Jessie and Amy's party, Elizabeth queried every person she trusted about how to help a Saudi girl in immanent danger of family retribution. Her immediate circle of acquaintances
~~~

knew of her debacle but was unable to offer any solutions that could work for a Saudi girl.

Chapter 16

Tansy

Before she spent any more time on trying to find the safest abortifacient, Elizabeth felt she should make sure that Amina was willing to cooperate. She remembered that Amina was from a seemingly very religious family. She lived in a family of mostly women but if they were so religious, she might not be willing to tempt Allah to kill a fetus. This was not *jihad* and as far as Elizabeth had been able to discover so far *jihad* referred only to striving against the enemies of Islam. It was probably unlikely that her family would assist Amina in destroying the fetus. However, one never knew what lurked in the hearts and minds of old women who had seen much.

Elizabeth feared that Amina might not come to class in case her situation upset her so much she believed she was doomed. But she dragged into class looking paler than usual. Though she still wore a very unique green silk blouse, her demeanor was not that of the proud beauty she had displayed at the beginning of the semester. At the end of the lecture class period Elizabeth asked her to stay and help set up some plastic body models before they started the next laboratory. While they were alone, she said, "I have an idea for you. Can you stay after the laboratory so we can talk alone?"

She had just gotten Amina's agreement to stay when her other two classmate came frolicking back in apparently unaware of Amina's distress. Elizabeth thought this was good.

When the laboratory reviewing the heart muscles was finally over, Amina said she had to go to the restroom and told her classmates not to wait for her. When she returned to the nursing laboratory classroom, she said, "What idea, Mrs. Elizabeth? I am despairing!"

"Come and sit down," Elizabeth said, indicating two chairs she had moved to the middle of the room in case anyone would try to listen outside the door. She wanted their conversation to be far enough from the doorway to avoid a passerby listening. She had thought of taking this conversation out to the fountain in the Administration Building courtyard but nobody went outside for more than a minute during the middle of the day unless they had to, even in December in the desert. "Amina, there are solutions called abortifacients which can sometimes cause women to abort a fetus. Would you consider trying something like that?"

She slowly raised her eyes to meet Elizabeth. For the first time since she had come to Elizabeth to ask for her help, Amina's face lit up in hope. It was the first time she had not looked either terrified or condemned since she had first beseeched Elizabeth for help. "Yes, yes. I try," she said.

"Amina, it can be very dangerous to a woman to use an abortifacient. I know of several different plants that can be used to help a woman start her period. In the past some women have used them to get rid of a fetus," Elizabeth explained. She had decided to use only the word fetus, not 'baby' hoping that would cause Amina to think of it as a thing, not as a person.

"Mrs. Elizabeth you know I desperate. I try quinine and nothing happen. I do anything now. If my family know I pregnant and not married, my brothers and father kill me."

"Does anyone in your family suspect you now?" Elizabeth inquired.

"I not think so," Amina said doubtfully. "I not sure. My sister Fatimah getting married. Nobody pay attention to me."

"Do you want me to try to find an abortifacient for you since the quinine did not work?" asked Elizabeth.

"Yes, please, I try anything. I die anyway if not work." Amina wrung her hands which were bereft of the usual jewels.

"Before I look for the right recipe and ingredients are you sure that Dr. Maloof will not come back and marry you?" Wishing to avoid participating in this chancy abortion, Elizabeth wanted to try every other alternative.

"No, he will not come back. They kill him too if they know. Besides he do not love me." Amina lowered her head toward her chest and tears appeared on her cheeks. "I thought he loved me but he say 'no.'"

"OK, let me find the right herbs. Where can you stay while the medicine works?" Elizabeth asked.

"I can no tell anybody, family or friend. Can I stay in hotel? If another woman with me, I can check into hotel."

"OK, I'll check in to the hotel with you but I may not be able to stay the whole time. But I will help you." Elizabeth felt she could not abandon this young woman at such a vulnerable time.

"Could I telephone to you at your house?" inquired Elizabeth.

"No, no, foreigner calling house make mother and father suspicious," Amina replied.

"Alright! Just stay after class each day and ask to help me set up the laboratory or say you need to ask a question. When I have found the herbs and a good recipe, then we will make plans for the hotel."

Amina's movements were still slow and depressed as she arose to put on her *abaya* to go to the gate for the guard to summon her driver.

~~~

Elizabeth became convinced that tansy was the safest of the herbs she had read about. How to find tansy in Riyadh? David had mentioned that the maintenance man in his USA Army Consultants' Compound had a green house out in the back corner. Maybe he could help find some. The maintenance man was from the Philippines and probably had a bunch of friends who also tended green houses. Also a Filipino would not be apt to turn anybody in for anything as they almost all felt vulnerable and wanted to avoid anything with the police.

Or could the little flower bed at University Administration Building which was kept looking like an English garden with a profusion of flowering plants possibly have tansy?
~~~

Elizabeth had been surprised to see such flowering abundance in the heat of the desert. She waited until everyone from the Nursing Department had gone for afternoon rest time before she took her copy of *Encyclopedia of Herbs and their Uses* out to compare the picture of tansy with the blossoms and leaves in the Administration flower bed. She put on her *abaya* so she would appear to be ready to be on her way home.

There they were, the bright yellow flower blossoms in the back. They looked like big marigolds which were also there but in the front row. These two yellow blossom plants were separated by some blue bachelor buttons. Elizabeth looked around the courtyard. In the heat of the afternoon no one but herself was visible in the courtyard. The ground in the flowerbed was still wet from recent watering. A hose lay nearby.

Surreptitiously, hoping she was not observed, trying to check if she herself was observed, Elizabeth glanced around and looked up at the few windows which gave unto the courtyard. Everyone must be having their afternoon nap, she surmised. She allowed the *abaya* to fall open so she could draw out her bandage scissors from her skirt pocket.

The recipe she had read for the tisane, called for leaves or flowers, however, she considered it better to take some of the stalk too. She snipped the biggest stalk with had several blossoms and flowers and swept it inside her *abaya* as she dropped the scissors back inside her pocket. There were still several stalks so she hoped the one she took would not be missed.

With this accomplished she allowed her body to feel the afternoon winter sun beating on her through her black *abaya.* Inside back in her office, she secreted the stalk of tansy in a plastic bag she had saved for this purpose. Then she slid the flattened stalk in between some professional papers she hoped to read soon. Her briefcase should keep the stalk somewhat cool until she could put it into the refrigerator in the flat. Elizabeth considered what she should say to Ina; she still felt she did not know Ina well enough to trust her with this plan to assist Amina.

At the bus stop, she flattened herself against the wall to get as much out of the afternoon sun as possible. Buses in the afternoon were unpredictable. But she did not have to wait too long. Grateful for the air-conditioning in the bus, she sagged into the seat being the only occupant of the women's section at this hour.

After considering whether she needed to conceal the tansy, she decided it would be safest. She got off the bus a few blocks before the flat and went into a small food market and bought a head of celery. Walking the few blocks to the flat even in the winter, the sun was challenging but she had also bought a bottle of Pepsi to keep her from heat exhaustion. She had drunk several gulps before leaving the air-conditioning of the store. It was enough so she felt she was splashing inside as she hurried home.

As usual Ina's door was closed so Elizabeth took the plastic bag with the tansy from her briefcase and slipped the celery stalk inside. When she had first arrived in August, Ina had told her which shelves and which hydrator drawer she could use. No negotiating! Since she had been made to feel somewhat like an intruder at first, Elizabeth had simple accepted what was assigned. Now she was grateful for having been assigned the lower shelves and the drawer closest to the refrigerator door hinges as it was easer to conceal what was in the drawer. She made sure that the celery stalks completely covered the tansy.

She had found a recipe for making the tisane of tansy but she wanted to try it when she was sure Ina would not be coming to use the kitchen. Ina often went out for several hours each evening. She had never shared where she went or with whom. But her evening schedule was fairly predictable, so Elizabeth planned to wait until she left for her usual evening absence. Also, Elizabeth felt she must try some of the concoction before allowing Amina to drink it. If Amina was to be poisoned, in the process, so would she be.

As soon as she heard Ina depart and lock the door, Elizabeth hurried to the kitchen. She put the full teakettle on the stove burner and washed the tansy with cool soapy water the same way she had learned it was necessary to wash all produce here. After rinsing, she patted it dry with the kitchen towel and stripped some leaves, not all, as she might need to try another batch. She decided to try the flowers in a separate steeping. There was no ceramic teapot in the flat so she took out one of the glass mixing bowls, put the tansy leaves in and slightly crushed them against the bowl. When the teakettle came to a boil she poured it covering the leaves and setting a ceramic plate on top of the bowl to keep the heat in as long as possible.

It was still a few days before Elizabeth was due to have her period, so she decided to see if the tea would bring it on early as the herb book suggested it would. Tomorrow was Thursday so she would have the weekend to either recover from bringing on her period early or to die trying. So after ten minutes, she lifted the plate and dipped a coffee cup into the brew, leaving another perhaps two cups worth in the bowl to cool. It tasted slightly bitter, so she added some honey and drank it down. Then she went to bed and struggled to sleep, finally slipping off when she did not expect it. She had decided to wear a kotex pad to bed just in case the tansy worked as she hoped it would.

Indeed, she awoke during the night feeling the wetness between her legs. She arose from the poly-foam palette and crossed the hallway to the bathroom. By the time she pulled her panties down to sit on the toilet, she was flooding blood from her vagina. And she felt pretty sick. She doubled over as she sat on the toilet seat and put her head between her knees.

CHAPTER 20

AMINA

As planned, Amina stayed after class the following Saturday and puttered with the plastic anatomy models while Fairuz and Mouna donned their *abayas*.

"Mrs. Adams, Can you explain me the lungs again?" she asked as a cover for her real reason.

Fairuz remarked as they departed loud enough so both Elizabeth and Amina heard her "American's have word 'teacher's pet.' Amina try to be teacher's pet!" She smirked at Amina before disappearing.

Amina was more disturbed by Fairuz's demeanor than by her words as she was so perennially anxious now so that English words mattered less than the feeling she got from watching her classmates, envious of her relationship with the teacher. As soon as she felt sure they were gone, she stood beseechingly in front of Elizabeth. "You have tea?"

"Yes, I made some of the tea. I did not bring it today but I will bring it to the hotel. Which hotel because we need to do this as soon as possible? The longer we wait, the more dangerous it is for you." She did not include that it would also be dangerous for Elizabeth herself. She did not want to add to Amina's anxiety and guilt.

"I will come to University Hospital and call to your flat. Then we take taxi together to Riyadh Palace Hotel," explained Amina.

"We need to do that on Wednesday evening so that you have two days to recover before returning to class. How will you explain your absence to your family?" said Elizabeth.

"I already tell them I make friends with Mouna and she asked me to stay her house sometime. They meet Mouna but no have telephone number. I just tell them I stay her house," replied Amina.

"What if they ask you to give her phone number?" questioned Elizabeth.

"I just tell them 'wrong number.' If they try call, I say I make mistake," Amina confessed how she would lie.

~~~

Amina was seated on the floor against the lobby wall in the hospital. There were a number of other black clad figures squatting against the wall, too. But Amina's exquisitely embroidered *abaya* stood out even here among all these black figures. She immediately arose when she saw her teacher. Elizabeth had covered her face which she usually did not do, but she and Amina had discussed that it would be better if people did not see her with a foreigner. Elizabeth's height among these Arab women was distinguishing but with a covered face, they could not be sure. For this short time, Elizabeth could see some worth in having a face covering.

As they got into the first taxi in the line outside the hospital, Amina did all the talking, lest Elizabeth give away
~~~

her foreign identity. So they sat quietly for the ride to the Riyadh Palace Hotel.

They drove under the flaring façade which had the name of the hotel in both Arabic and English in three dimensional lettering. This façade provided more shade than hotel entrances Elizabeth was familiar with in the USA.

The front door attendant opened the back door of the taxi and Elizabeth exited while Amina paid the driver. Amina swept up to the registration desk as if she had done this before. With her exquisite clothing as a foil, she was treated as Elizabeth supposed the Royal Family might be. The attendant at the 'check in desk' was dressed in Western street clothes so it was difficult to know which nationality he was. Men in the street were easily distinguishable by the color of their *ghutra*. Since he and Amina were speaking Arabic, Elizabeth could not tell whether he had an accent or not. She promised to ask Amina later what nationality he was. Amina slid a stack of *riyals*, Saudi currency, across the desk.

The lobby of the Riyadh Palace Hotel was as gaudily decorated as one could wish for like an Ali Baba cave with rich upholstery of Arabic design, side and coffee tables both sturdy and gaudy mixing marble and glass at the same time, glorious chandelier lighting fixtures and carpets deserving of royal feet.

The desk clerk motioned for the bellhop to approach the desk. Each woman had an overnight bag while Elizabeth carried an additional small suitcase. Elizabeth had concealed the plastic water bottle with the tansy tea in her small suitcase as well as pajamas, a package of kotex, rubber surgery sheet, and a blood pressure cuff. Her own menses had ceased but the extra package of kotex was for Amina in case she had not completed the abortion by the time they were scheduled to leave the hotel.

Elizabeth wondered if people viewing them would think she was Amina's servant since her own *abaya* and face cloth were so plain compared to Amina's fancily edged cloak. As long as the girl was treating her like a savior and not a servant, Elizabeth did not care. In fact, they probably looked more authentically Saudi Arabia with the rich young woman accompanied by a servant.

The bellhop was appropriately obsequious to Amina, ignoring Elizabeth, probably assuming that she was a servant. He led them to the elevator carrying Amina's overnight kit but ignoring Elizabeth's so she carried it herself as she preferred that anyway.She could hear the tansy tea splashing inside the bottle in the small case. She had not planned to appear as Amina's servant but now that the situation presented itself, she judged it to be a useful disguise.

It was not just a hotel room; it was a suite with a parlor and bath, kitchenette/bar and bedroom. The bar was supplied with only soft drinks, of course but it had all the right drink mixes if someone brought in their own illegal liquor. Both bedroom and parlor had huge TVs. Prayer rugs hung over the backs of the arm chairs. Again the décor mimicked 'desert at sunset' colors. Elizabeth was grateful for the kitchenette as she had anticipated having to use the bathroom sink for cleaning up any blood. There was the inevitable hat tree inside the entry door for hanging *abayas*.

As soon as they had placed their cases in the bedroom

twirled the rings on her fingers, "I promise not to throw myself under a truck until we try everything. Let me tell you about my sister's wedding, as that might keep my mind off my trouble," Amina replied. "I happy for her."

Elizabeth encouraged her to keep sipping the tansy tisane.

"Fatimah engaged to Abdul for almost a year. He works with Father in the ministry. His specialty is finance so he doesn't exactly work with Father but he work in accounting department. My father like him and so when he and Mother thought it was time for Fatimah to find husband, Father suggest Abdul. Abdul interested and he discuss it with his family. So they had meeting. They made us all go upstairs with Aunt Maymunah."

Talking about this did seem to distract Amina from the business at hand as Elizabeth had to remind her to keep sipping. About two thirds of the glass was drunk. Elizabeth had taken one of the Pepsis from the refrigerator and sipped it along with Amina.

"Abdul like Fatimah after they were left alone for half an hour to talk together. She like him, too. The families signed engagement agreement. Then they call us other children down to meet him. We celebrate with coffee and pastries. Then they left. Fatimah was both sad and happy, too."

Elizabeth reminded her to drink it to the dregs. She still had as much left in the liter bottle sitting on the bar as Amina had already drunk.

"Fatimah began planning for her wedding. Both Mother and Aunt and Grandmother began to help her gather her, how do you call it, trousseau?"

"How do you feel now? Let me take your blood pressure again. I will have something to compare with the one we already took and then again later," Elizabeth said as she got up and reached for the cuff.

"I don't feel sleepy yet. I have not sleep well since this." Amina patted her abdomen. "So wedding is in a month. I happy for Fatimah."

Elizabeth wondered how happy she really was for her sister, since Amina herself was so miserable. But she decided it was not the time for this discussion so she said, "Just finish the tea while you tell me about the wedding plans and then go to bed. Be sure to put on a kotex and kotex belt before you lie down." Elizabeth wondered if she herself would be able to go to sleep or if her anxiety about what they were doing, about Amina would allow her to sleep. And perhaps she should not sleep in case something happened to Amina and she did not recognize it. "I will sit by your bed until you go to sleep," she reassured the girl.

"If I live, I like you come Fatimah's wedding," Amina said as she set the empty glass down.

"I am sure you will live. I would like very much to come to the wedding. But now sleep," as she led Amina toward the bedroom promising to rinse out the tansy glass in case anything happened and there was evidence to hide.

Elizabeth lay down on the other bed closer to the window which looked out across the city. Sounds of traffic still drifted through windows which were sealed to keep out sand and dry desert winds. People of Riyadh had much night life if one judged by the traffic rather than the remembering the restrictions about banned music and entertainments. For young men, driving and racing cars on night streets was a common entertainment, Elizabeth had learned.

She awoke to groans. Amina was groaning in Arabic so Elizabeth was unsure of the exact words. But the feeling was explicit. The girl was in pain, obviously in the process of aborting the fetus.

Elizabeth arose and went to the door and turned on the lights. She could see Amina writhing on the bed. She was glad she had insisted that she put the rubber sheet under her. "Amina, do you want to go to the toilet?" she said as she reached out to pull back the bedcovers.

The only response was "Aye, aye aye, oh."

Elizabeth could see blood on the rubber sheet under Amina who clutched her abdomen. "Let me help you to the toilet," Elizabeth said as she grasped Amina's hand and pulled at the rubber sheet to the same time.

Amina allowed herself to be pulled to the edge of the bed and upright. There was a pool of blood on the rubber sheet which ran down the side of the fitted bottom sheet as Amina arose and leaned on Elizabeth. They lumbered together toward the bathroom and the toilet dripping a trail of blood. Amina sat down hard on the toilet seat letting out another moan. Elizabeth could see muscle contraction in her slender abdomen as Amina tried to lessen the pain by folding her body over with her head between her knees and then raring back against the toilet seat cover. Elizabeth rolled up a towel and put one end of the roll in Amina's hands and told her to pull while Elizabeth pulled back as well. Groans accompanied each pull. Elizabeth was fearful that the girl might be hemorrhaging rather than just expelling the fetus but she wanted her to completely eject the entire thing so she would not end up with an infection from any remaining tissue.

Eventually, the seeming contractions of her slender abdomen stopped and she began to cry. Meanwhile Elizabeth started to wipe up the blood on the tile floor. She allowed Amina to just sit on the toilet until she straightened up and reached for toilet paper. Elizabeth brought her another kotex pad to replace the completely soaked one that had fallen on the bathroom floor. "Don't flush it. Let me look at what came out," Elizabeth ordered. "Be sure and wipe your feet so you don't track any more blood on the carpet." Elizabeth knew she already had quite a job to sponge all the dripped blood out of the carpet.

After Amina wiped herself, Elizabeth assisted her to stand and guided her back to the other bed putting a towel under her in case the kotex did not absorb the remaining blood. She handed Amina a hot cup of regular tea from the teapot she had left on brewing on the bar counter.

Returning to the toilet, the water was so bloody that she could not see to the bottom so she reached her hand in and felt the slimy cluster of tissue. She had to use both hands to keep it from slipping back into the toilet. Watery bloody fluid dripped on the floor as she took the tissue to the sink to examine it. Laying it gently in the sink, she rinsed the blood off so she could examine it. It was indeed colorless flesh, a scimitar shaped cluster of cells about four inches long and half an inch thick. Elizabeth judged that there had been a complete abortion. Only blood was left in the uterus, no other tissue to cause infection. She gave a great sigh of relief as she flushed the cell mass down the toilet.

Then she set about cleaning up, washing her hands, wetting a washcloth and sponging blood from the places she had dripped on the carpet. Since she had put Amina in her own bed, she carefully took up the rubber sheet, folding up the corners to avoid dripped any more blood on the carpet and rinsing it off in the bathtub. Then she took off the bottom sheet and rinsed out where blood had dripped on it when Amina stood up. She emptied out the rest of the tansy tea, rinsed the bottle and put it in the waste basket.

By now, Amina was sleeping so Elizabeth sat down on the sofa in the parlor and let her whole body tremble as the tension finally left her. Of course, they were not 'out of the woods' yet she reminded herself. She had to see by check out time at noon tomorrow, whether Amina was sufficiently recovered to get into a taxi to go home. She could miss a few days at school but she could not miss more days away from her family.

Chapter 21

Wedding

Due to her youth and general good health, Amina had recovered quickly so they were able to check out of the Riyadh Palace Hotel before noon. She looked pale but not remarkably so. Besides, her face was covered as they departed the suite. Before leaving, Elizabeth had examined the room to make sure there were no remnants of the abortion left in the waste basket. She wrapped all the bloody paper towels, kotex etc. inside one of the rubber sheets and put it inside a plastic bag inside her own suitcase to dispose of in her own flat.

When the taxi stopped in front of the hospital, Amina promised to send a car for Elizabeth to pick her up for Fatimah's wedding the following weekend. It would be held at a different hotel ballroom. Amina had made sure their recent episode had been at a different hotel so that there was no chance of the hotel staff recognizing her despite having been covered at all times outside the hotel room.

The following week of classes was unremarkable except that in nursing lab, despite looking a little pale under her olive complexion, Amina was able to vividly describe in detail for her classmates the preparations for Fatimah's wedding; the dresses, the henna hand artist, the hair-removal waxing, the musicians, the caterer, the men's party which would be held in yet another ballroom, and the flower girls.

For Elizabeth a conundrum was – what to wear? She had discussed her invitation to the wedding with Amy and Jessie to discover if there were any protocols that would affect her. Having been here several years already, they had both been to several weddings and suggested that she wear her dressiest dress. Her dressy dresses were all short dresses back in California. She had brought only blouses and long skirts to Saudi Arabia. However, Amy suggested that she look in the booth in the souq where there were prepackaged caftans that needed only to be hemmed and sewed up the sides. Amy volunteered to take her to that particular booth. There she found a rust colored rayon satin caftan kit that had an arrangement of gold embroidery around the neckline interspersed with red sequins. All she would have to do is follow the instructions in Arabic to cut out and face the neckline before stitching up the side seams. The diagram was understandable without English explanation. Elizabeth had been sewing since she was ten years old with her Aunt Sephrena and Aunt Phyllis so she felt she did not need instructions in either Arabic or English.

Then they went to the gold souq where Elizabeth bought a pair of English gold half-crown earrings like the one she had admired on the cleaning woman at the nursing department. She was already thinking about money in *riyals* instead of dollars.

By the time Elizabeth had sewed up the caftan, put her hair up using combs and hair pins, with her red-gold hair and gold earrings against her slender neck, she looked quite elegant, according to Amy. "You will be quite presentable to these Saudi ladies," Amy promised.

The car and Filipino driver appeared as promised as well. She felt quite small and alone in the backseat of the maroon Chrysler New Yorker. The driver had picked her up on the street in front of the flats instead of at the hospital. She felt it was a shame her elegant dress was covered by her *abaya*. Gingerly, she had covered her swept-up hairdo but had not covered her face so the driver knew who to look for despite the ubiquitous black *abaya*.

He dropped her off under the hotel port cochere about eight o'clock. There was quite line of cars dropping off women in *abayas*. She intended to go to the hotel clerk to ask where the wedding was, but Amina had apparently been awaiting her and called out, "Mrs. Elizabeth." She took her arm and they got into the line of black clad women flowing toward a ballroom, except such a room was called a 'banquet room' since Saudis did not have rooms named 'ballrooms' as it implied men and women dancing together. Inside the banquet room, they were greeted by Mrs. Khoury and the groom's mother. Amina introduced her teacher to them. The room was full of women. Amina seated Elizabeth near the front of the room by her teenage sisters. They removed their *abayas*. Amina seemed fully recovered from her abortion ordeal and was dressed in a gorgeous red silk ball-gown which could have come out of *Gone with the Wind*. Eagerly she introduced Elizabeth to two of her younger sisters. Amina explained that her youngest sister, along with several cousins would be flower girls and were in an upstairs suite being dressed and prepared for their entrance. The room was in an uproar with women removing their *abayas*, face veils and greeting friends and relatives. They gave the three kiss greetings, a kiss on one cheek, a kiss on the other and a third kiss on the first cheek.

The dresses, as they unwrapped themselves from their *abayas*, were fancier than Americans wore to Christmas parties, with mountains of sequins, glitter, gold embroidery and covered with gold jewelry so that Elizabeth felt quite out-shown compared to how she had felt when she had looked at herself in the mirror in the bathroom back at the flat. She noticed that several women wore the kind of gold necklace that is like a chain mail bib of gold from neck to waist. Others wore a kind of glove of gold that actually was a series of rings on each finger and a wrist band connected to each ring by gold chains which had a jewel encrusted disc on each link. The women all kept their black face veils handy. The moment a man came in to bring more chairs, up went the face clothes, sometimes sideways to shield just the side of the face toward the man. The children, and there were batches of them, were all dressed up too; the girls in miniature wedding dresses, made Elizabeth think they were practicing for their future weddings. Some black serving women came in carrying huge trays of cups for Arabic coffee which in this case was really just cardamom and saffron, not coffee at all.

The band arrived about nine o'clock. It was an 'all women' band with the leader playing an instrument like a large mandolin called an *ude*. The rest of the band played percussion instruments and sang. Amina, who after greeting a number of relatives, came to sit beside Elizabeth, explained that they were 'love songs!' Every time a serving man came into the room, the musicians got their face clothes up without missing a beat. The seven musicians played like mad with a black cloth wrapped completely around and over each face, while they sat on the stage and sang into microphones. After most guests had arrived, the two mothers came and sat on the front row in front of Amina, and her sisters. Elizabeth enjoyed the music.

About 10:45 pm, the wedding procession came in led by twelve little girls in the miniature white wedding dresses, carrying huge flaming white tapers. Elizabeth immediately began to worry lest one of them light her hair or dress on fire. Once they got into place on either side of the bridal couple who had entered after them, and the photographer finished, they put the tapers out and Elizabeth breathed a sigh of relief. No one else seemed to have been worried. The bride dressed in a traditional western type white wedding dress and the groom dressed in a finely tucked white Saudi *thobe* with white *ghutra* and black *igal*, sat up on a stage in two big carved upholstered chairs surrounded with artificial flowers. A couple of relatives came up and gave gold to the bride. Then the groom opened a brief case and took out one of those gold bibs and put it around Fatimah's neck. That was it! The ceremony was over. The real signing of marriage contracts had taken place in another banquet room where the males of both families witnessed the legality. So the wedding was already completed before Fatimah and her new husband entered the women's party banquet room.

The wedding couple got up and went out and led the others into another banquet room where about twenty square yards of table were solidly covered with food. The wedding guests followed the couple into the feast. Within twenty minutes, the table was a shambles of half filled plates, overturned Pepsi cans and empty serving vessels. The bridal couple had by then disappeared.

Amina and her younger sisters donned their *abayas* and

face veils and went to the lobby to help put Elizabeth into a taxi and send her home to her flat.

Amina whispered to Elizabeth as they parted, "Since Fatimah's married, my mother and father are looking for a husband for me."

As Elizabeth looked out at night-time Riyadh passing by the sedan window, she remembered conversations she had heard about non-virgins being rejected and sent back to their families if they did not bleed on their wedding night.

Chapter 22

Confidences

Unable to confide in Jessie and Amy, whom she had come to trust in most Saudi social situations, Elizabeth decided to unload her anxieties about the Amina episode with David Nelson. She called and said "I heard from your mother. She says meet her in Jareer Street."

David responded "Tell my mother to meet me at 4 PM in Jareer Street."

Elizabeth knew this was code for confirming the meeting at the *falafel* stand. She decided that her nervous energy might be worked off if she walked the entire route, rather than taking a taxi or bus. As she walked slowly to avoid overheating and dehydration, she contemplated the issues to discuss with David. She just wanted to relieve her own anxiety by talking to a trusted friend and she had come to trust David. She could not put any of these anxieties on paper in a letter to Graham Brown or her girlfriends back in California. She had learned that all mailing addresses and return addresses were photocopied by the secretary Amal and sent to the Dean. She could not be sure that some mail was not opened and read as well, though she have never seen evidence of it on envelopes she received. Therefore, she felt she could only express her anxieties face to face as she suspected the telephones of foreigners were tapped as well.

As she rounded the corner, she saw David's jeep parallel parked in a line of cars beside the fourteen inch curb near the *falafel* stand. Then she saw David at the *falafel* stand ordering a cone of the succulent fried chickpea dumplings. The smell of the bubbling grease in the tub permeated the area. He held the cone out to her as she approached. For this trip, she had worn only her *abaya* as required but rather than the black *hijab*, she had worn a sunhat with a wide brim to protect from the desert sun during her walk. Hoping that observers would think they were a foreign husband and wife, David guided her without touching her, as husbands and wife did not touch in public in Saudi Arabia, toward the nearby covered vegetable produce market. But they both continued to munch on *falafel*.

When they were out of range for any of the shoppers or shop keepers to hear, as they walked, Elizabeth began her litany of anxieties, "Amina has learned that now that her older sister is safely married, her parents are looking for a husband for her as she must marry before her teenage sisters can marry."

"Yes, I've heard that that is the custom, for siblings to wait for their older brothers and sisters to marry before they ask their parents to marry," David replied.

Elizabeth went on to recount the difficulties this held for Amina. "Since she is no longer a virgin, she could be rejected on her wedding night and sent back to her family where they possibly would kill her. Or she could somehow get to Egypt and have the surgery for hymen repair. Right now, I can't think of any other options that would not flout

Saudi mores."

"Let's go back to my flat where we can discuss this in more privacy without worrying if anybody near us understands English," said David.

Again, there was nobody in the compound gatehouse. "Is there ever anybody minding this gate?" she asked.

"There's seldom anybody here because we're all US Army except some AWAC pilots stay here when they are not flying." David explained.

They delayed anymore talk about Amina's situation until they were inside David's villa. "When I moved in here, I went over the whole place looking for microphones. I do it again every so often just to make sure they are not listening into my private conversations. I know it seems kind of paranoid, but these Saudis have no bounds when it comes to monitoring foreigner's behavior. If anybody asks about you, I'll just lie and say you are my wife. I couldn't say you are my sister because they know they probably wouldn't give my sister a visa to visit so if I said that, it would be suspect. Besides, the Army doesn't want to bring anybody but wives here as dependents anyway. Most of these security people for our compound are also foreigners and they don't particularly want to cooperate with the Saudis anyway." As he talked, David poured some California wine, something Elizabeth had not seen for months. "We just got our 'furniture shipment,'" David explained with a smile as he handed her the glass.

As they settled onto the sofa beside each other, David went on, "I've heard of non-virgins faking it by inserting a plastic bag of sheep's blood in their vagina on their wedding night. If I were the groom, I think I would probably be able to tell the difference, but if the guy is a virgin, too, he might not realize it wasn't her broken hymen that was bleeding."

"This wine tastes so good. It's so long since I tasted a nice California rose'," Elizabeth said as she sipped. She turned toward David and kissed his lips, tasting the wine in his mouth, too.

He slipped his arms around her and began to stroke her back and neck. "What do you say; shall we flout some more Saudi rules by going in the bedroom and taking off our clothes?" He set his wine glass on the coffee table and tugged at her arm. "I have something to celebrate. I've heard from Claire's lawyer. He sent the final divorce papers for me to sign."

The wine had reduced inhibitions even though Elizabeth still felt a little alarm about conceiving despite knowing David was careful about birth-control. It was wonderful to feel desired and safely cocooned in this American Army compound villa. The original reason for this tryst diminished as desire overcame fear.

As they returned to the living room after making love, a more relaxed Elizabeth said, "Maybe we are getting ahead of ourselves as Amina's parents are apparently still asking friends and family about possible husbands for her. They still haven't invited any to come over for the prescribed family meeting."

"OK, but it's still good to discuss possibilities as you really seem to have taken as a project saving the life of this student," David replied.

"Amina has mentioned that there is a first cousin that

she has been told since she was a child, that he would be a good husband for her. They were playmates before she put on their veil, but he has been away in the States getting his degree in petroleum engineering so she hasn't seen him in years. He'll be home soon." Elizabeth stood and said, "It's probably time for me to get back. You haven't had enough wine to get caught by the Saudi traffic police, have you?"

"Nah, you may be out of practice, but I usually have a drink every night before I go to bed. But I'll use mouthwash before I drive you back," he said as he turned toward the bathroom to follow words with actions.

It was still early enough in the evening that there were no Saudi traffic police in view as there would be later when the young Saudi men, full of testosterone with no place to expend it, raced each other up and down Airport Road.

Lying on her foam mattress alone later, Elizabeth contemplated why she never thought of Graham Brown anymore, nor did she feel guilty about sleeping with David. She wondered if she was the only Western woman flouting the Saudi's strict rule about unmarried sex. The mores about unmarried sex in the USA had loosened so much in the last decade that she could not imagine that she was the only Western woman taking these risks. She had so much more freedom of movement than the Filipina and Korean nurses and physical therapists that lived in the hospital staff hostels. She remember the case that one of the nurses had told about a Korean nurse who on her every two weeks half-day trip to the *souq*, had met her Korean boyfriend who took her for a ride in his car and had an accident, causing both of them to be immediately deported home, thus losing their livelihood as prescribed by their government labor contract.

If she could only persuade Amina to try to flee to another country maybe she could get David's help in forging documents and smuggling her out, but Amina has refused to reject her family and their rules. She loves her family even though she knew she broke their rules, both by having sex outside marriage and aborting the resulting fetus. She doesn't want to die but she loves her family enough to keep risking death at their hands. She was conscious that the more time Amina spent with her, the more she seemed to want to live and was more willing to take risks. Elizabeth had wanted to ask Amina why she took the risk of letting Dr. Mahmoud Maloof make love to her, but she could not be sure that such a spirited girl as Amina had not lured Dr. Maloof instead of the other way around. Finally these tautological thoughts succumbed to fatigue and she slipped into a troubled sleep.

Chapter 23

What Next?

The sharing of the dangerous abortion experience had created a bond between Amina and her teacher. Elizabeth had certainly not intended that kind of relationship when she embarked on her 'savior role' as she knew it compromised her role as teacher. But now that that danger was past and another ahead for Amina with her missing hymen, Elizabeth felt she could not abandon her. Amina had grown to trust her almost as a family member, though how she could trust family members who might kill her for honor baffled Elizabeth.

Amina found reasons to stay after lecture and lab almost every session. Her classmates at first had chided her about being 'Teacher's Pet' but they gradually accepted it. Usually Amina assumed the 'ignorant student' pose as if she needed extra tutoring. This was not hard to affect as the other two, Fairuz and Mouna did seem to be better students. However, Amina reminded them often of her dedication to the profession of nursing inspired by her experience of being with her grandmother before she died.

Occasionally, Mouna volunteered to study with Amina which complicated Amina's attempts to stay behind to talk to Elizabeth. Usually, Amina found some excuse to stay with her teacher in the nursing laboratory such as needing to use the lab equipment or to study the plastic models which were better than drawings in the textbook.

It occurred to Elizabeth to wonder why she had never questioned Amina about whether Fairuz knew or suspected more about her relationship with her brother, Mahmoud, since she had had a part in facilitating their meeting. Well, Elizabeth excused herself that she was new to this country and culture and had been on a sharp learning curve, thus was not aware of all the nuances or her students' lives but she should have known about that particular aspect of this situation. She promised herself to question Amina about this next time they were alone. Surely their assistance in making excuses for Amina or distracting Elizabeth had made them suspect more about the relationship than was evident now. Amina had not invited either of her classmates to her sister's wedding. Perhaps there was a clue in that situation to explain why her classmates had been unaware of the direness of her recent situation. After Mahmoud had fled to England, undoubtedly, Amina struggled to keep the consequences of that adventure from his sister and consequently from his family, who like her own family would have felt obligated to extract some kind of Islamic justice, perhaps not as drastic as would have been applied to Amina. She had apparently cared about Mahmoud, but not enough to sacrifice herself, just to sacrifice the fetus.

During the after class 'study sessions' with Elizabeth, Amina occasionally slipped and expressed thoughts bordering on suicidal because of the seeming hopelessness of her situation. Elizabeth worked strenuously to assure her of positive thoughts and hopes. Perhaps if she finished her nursing degree, she could apply to go to America to get her master's in nursing and come back and teach here. Could she begin to discuss such a plan with her parents? But she had no brother or uncle who could be sent out of the country with her to be her guardian as was required by law. Her father certainly could not abandon his job and her sisters to do so even if her mother would allow him to go. The simplest way would be for her to marry some other college graduate who wanted to go aboard to finish his education. But to do that was to subject her to the possibility of him discovering she was not a virgin.

Who would want a beautiful young capable professional wife without a hymen? An old man might want a second or third wife but then he would not leave his other wives to accompany her to America. And besides, she would not be a widow or a divorcee as most second or third wives without hymens might be. Amina was a despoiled woman.

David spent time with Saudi soldiers and their officers. Maybe he might have some idea of different Saudi men than all the stereotypes Elizabeth had seen and heard or read about. She, herself, had little knowledge of Saudi men as she had assiduously avoided them on advice from Amy and Jessie when she first arrived, except for obligatory meetings with the Dean and doctors in the hospital. Most of the men such as salesmen she spoke to in the souq were foreigners such as Egyptians or Pakistanis. The carpet sellers were usually Saudis but they were almost the only ones.

Was it too soon to call David again and ask him to meet? Would he be old-fashioned and think she was pursuing him? Should she call him and ask him by their code to meet her? Then she remembered that David also occasionally attended the Riyadh International Christian Fellowship.

Maybe she could persuade him to pick her up for church. Actions followed thoughts.

"David, this is Elizabeth. Your mother is fine but I am wondering if I could get a ride to RICF tomorrow?" She knew that anyone listening, if they were, would probably not understand the acronym for the Riyadh International Christian Fellowship if she said it fast enough.

"OK, I wasn't planning to go but since you need a ride, it will be a pleasure," he responded.

Now Elizabeth would have to explain to Jessie and Amy why she did not ride with them and Chuck to RICF. They liked David and seemed to have no negative thoughts about her seeing him. They just wanted her to be safe and not in jeopardy to Saudi laws and justice. After her conversation with David was finished, she called on the in-house phone to ask if she could come up to their flat for a visit.

She could smell the lovely aroma of cardamom coffee as she entered the door. The set of tiny cups with the Turkish stovetop coffee pot *dallah*, was on a wooden tray on the brass tray style coffee table. Jessie was obviously glad of company as she welcomed Elizabeth in and gestured for her to have a seat on the sofa.

Taking up her cup of cardamom coffee, Elizabeth started her explanation, "David Nelson has offered to drive me to RICF tomorrow. I wanted to be sure you knew that I won't need to ride with your folks and Chuck."

Amy smiled and lit a cigarette which she laid in the brass ashtray beside the coffee things. "Oh, we really like David. That's nice that he'll take you. I know how hard it is for women like you to get together with nice Western men here." She knew better than to offer Elizabeth a cigarette. Amy made sure the smoke drifted away from Elizabeth by waving it away.

Elizabeth chuckled inside to realize that Amy had no idea that she was as intimate with David as she had become. It was much easier than most people thought for Western men and women to get together in Riyadh. There were many more Western men here than women. Even older women like Jessie and Amy were often invited for hikes or group meals to keep lonely, homesick men company.

Friendship with younger women of her own generation who felt the same way about intimacy and sex was something that Elizabeth missed. She was very aware of the difference in values and mores between herself and these Southern nurses twenty years older. She missed being able to discuss such issues with a contemporary. There were a few women nearer her age at RICF but Elizabeth suspected that they were pretty straight-laced about sex and observing Islamic laws despite professing Christianity.

After the church service the next day, David took her for a drive to the town of Al-Kharj about fifty kilometers south of Riyadh. As they drove, sure that nobody could hear them, they were able to freely discuss how to outwit the Saudi attitude toward women, especially toward Amina. With Elizabeth covered in her *abaya* and newly acquired *niqab* and *hijab*, she sat in the front passenger seat of the jeep. With the eye-slits in the *niqab*, she did not miss any of the beautiful desert scenes, acacia trees, small herds of goats and camels, *wadis* with date palms.

"I want to help Amina get out of Saudi Arabia. She has to have a Saudi male guardian to get an exit visa and passport. They are so strict about it, I figure the only way she can do that is to get married, but as damaged goods, who will marry her without sending her back to her family when they realize she's not a virgin?" It felt strange talking with the black veil in front of her mouth.

"So what you are thinking about is helping Amina find a Saudi husband who won't care that she's no longer a virgin, yes?" confirmed David with a doubtful smile.

"Is there such a Saudi man, a Saudi man who wouldn't care if his new wife is not a virgin?" Elizabeth knew she was proposing an impossible Saudi man.

She went on, "I need to discuss this more with Amina, because there is no use in us trying to help her unless she's willing to accept the help," Elizabeth said as if talking to herself.

Chapter 29

What Does Amina Want

At the next possible opportunity, when Amina made an excuse to stay after laboratory class, Elizabeth inquired about her feelings about Westerners trying to help her find a husband who would accept her non-virgin state.

"I have no more excuse to say to parents why they not find me husband." She said this with apprehension.

This conversation took place over the plastic manikin on the hospital bed as they pretended to be practicing giving the plastic patient passive bed exercises. They talked as Amina moved the manikin's joints back and forth.

"It has to be a Saudi husband, yes? Your law says you can't marry a foreigner, doesn't it?" questioned Elizabeth.

"Yes, I no can marry Pakistani or Egyptian even if Muslim," Amina said with chagrin tinged with anger.

"Is there any kind of Saudi man who would not care that you are no longer a virgin? You need a Saudi male guardian if you leave this country. Is there anybody you know of who wants to go to graduate school abroad? Maybe we can trick them." Elizabeth wanted to give Amina a hopeful idea to think about.

"I do not know of any Saudi men like that. Every Saudi man want virgin first wife!" Amina was adamant.

Elizabeth reported what she had recently heard from one of her female Egyptian colleagues. "Mrs. Sohair told me that now sometimes professional women like nurses and doctors help each other meet prospective, that means possible husbands by giving phone numbers so they can talk and then they meet by some certain aisle in the supermarket. Do you know about that?"

"Yes, I hear about it. That how I want to meet Dr. Maloof, but he persuade me to go ride in car instead. He say it safe if we drove to desert." Amina finally explained how she got to be in a situation to be so easily seduced.

"So have you ever gone to meet anybody in the supermarket?" questioned Elizabeth while trying to discover how sophisticated Amina would be to meet men in a public place.

"No," said Amina, "but I know Mouna do it. She go meet Fairuz's other brother, ophthalmologist, but she no like him. She say he was too, hum, arrogant? I think that was word she say. Mouna is kind and she think he not kind."

"Would you be willing to go and meet a man that way?" asked Elizabeth.

"Yes, I do almost anything to find man to be guardian, to have husband who no care I not virgin." She said this in a whisper, looking at Elizabeth with hopeful eyes. "I really loved Mahmoud. But he no love me or he marry me." Tears ran down her brown cheeks. It was hard for Elizabeth not to fold her into an embrace: rather she simply stroked her arm.

Elizabeth almost never corrected her students' English language grammar lest she discourage them from trying to speak English, except when she did not understand what they meant. She was grateful that there were few situations where other English speakers could observe this as she was sure other faculty would feel she was not fulfilling her responsibility by not correcting them.

~~~

This time, Elizabeth asked David to meet her instead at the Jareer Street bookstore so they could then leave and find some other private place to talk. David had surprised her and arrived dressed in a *thobe, igal* and *ghutra*. He drove the jeep with Elizabeth scrunched in the back covered in her *abaya, niqab* and *hijab*. They both felt like folks dressed for a costume party except for the real danger of being stopped by the *mutawah* if they discovered an unmarried male and female together in a private vehicle. A traditional black Bedouin tent and camp with tethered camels was visible some distance from the highway. David drove the jeep to the old city ruins at Diriyah on the Wadi Hanifa, former home of the Saudi royal family and original capital. Now it was mostly broken mud walls. It had been the focal point of warring tribes for centuries. Now there were seldom any people there, especially Saudis. Elizabeth removed her *niqab* and *hijab* keeping her *abaya* pulled up over to conceal her red-brown hair.

As they walked among the ruins, Elizabeth recounted the conversation between herself and Amina. "How could I go about finding a man, perhaps a homosexual man who would like to go abroad where he is in less jeopardy than in Saudi Arabia? I don't suppose you ever meet anybody like that."
~~~

"As a matter of fact, Hamza, the Saudi National Guard officer I usually consult with has mentioned what to do with this one guy he suspects of being homosexual. The guy pretty much keeps to himself, does his job which is in inventory and supplies. Hamza has never caught him in the act, because apparently the guy never does anything in the barracks, but he says he has smelled his cologne. Of course, lots of Saudi men wear strong cologne, but apparently Hamza smelled something different about this guy."

"Is this somebody we could find out more about?" asked Elizabeth as they walked among the broken mud walls.

"You know it's hard to figure out in the Saudi National Guard if somebody is really a homosexual. Since all socializing with women except for immediate family is forbidden, these men are even more sex crazy than in the US Army if that's possible. They have all this pent up testosterone and sex drive and no place to get rid of it. So I am sure they do some homosexual acts just out of frustration. Determining whether or not they are really homosexual is chancy. But Hamza seems to be pretty enlightened. Let me have a talk with him about this situation. I'll see if I can find out more about this guy's family which may be more important than anything else."

"Do you have any other ideas about a type of man who might want to get out of Saudi?" questioned Elizabeth.

"Let's see if Hamza has any other ideas. I kind of trust his instincts. So far, whenever we're discussing troop practices, he seems to have an instinct for the best plan."

"Are there other professions like there are in the US such as airline stewards that have a lot of homosexual man in them?" asked Elizabeth, then she went on, "Some people think male nurses are often homosexual but that hasn't been my experience. In fact I don't believe in the places I've worked with a male nurse, that I ever knew one to be homosexual."

"Well, there's the proverbial myth that artists and museum directors are homosexuals but I don't know of any of them here. In fact I heard the lecture by the new Minister of Antiquities last month and he certainly did not strike me as anything near gay." They had reached the edge of the main ruins as David made this last statement.

As they headed back toward Central Riyadh, Elizabeth confirmed their plan with David, "So I'll just wait for you to talk to your friend Hamza. Should I say anything to Amina to give her hope?"

Steering around the broken mud walls, with Elizabeth safely confined in her *abaya, niqab* and *hijab* in the back seat, David suggested, "Why not ask Amina if she knows any homosexual men, cousins, uncles, guys who seem to like other men better than their families. She probably knows a lot more than she even realizes."

"I've hear the girls talk about matchmakers, *khatab*, I think they said." Elizabeth considered other ways of discovering possible ineligible men who could become eligible for Amina's purposes as she watched the city come into view.

David turned in the driver seat as he slowed the jeep, "Want to come help me celebrate the final divorce paper from Claire? They arrived yesterday."

This time as they passed the guard house, the little guy in the *thobe* and *ghutra* saluted David as they passed.

Chapter 28

Finding the Right Guy

While watching the fifteen minutes of English language evening news on television with David Nelson, Elizabeth saw the announcement on March 31, 1981 of the assassination attempt the day before on US President Ronald Reagan. This shocked all the American expatriates. It added to the winter gloom from rains over Riyadh. These rains make trips to the desert unpleasant. The Desert Ramblers took a hiatus from their weekend caravans of campers and hikers. Instead, they arranged for a group tour of the old Murraba Palace, the former residence of King Ibn Saud who had united the Kingdom. It was a two story mud structure entirely enclosing a stone flagged courtyard. All the rooms, including the King's audience hall, opened on to the portico which went around the courtyard. In the Audience Hall blue brocade carved and upholstered chairs lined the walls and sat in rows between the columns that were holding up the center of the room. The dated splendor of his court was very visible. Outside, from the parking lot one could see a rim of whitewashed crenellations along the roof line. The palace had been built in the 1930s. The group marveled at how well the mud had stood up.

Elizabeth had joined Amy and Jessie in Chuck Toiler's car to ride to the palace parking lot. As the tour guide from the Ministry of Antiquities led them around, David who had arrived alone, managed to stand near enough to Elizabeth to whisper to her that he had information on 'Cologne Man' which is the nickname they had given to the target husband since they did not know his real name. When the tour was over, Dr. and Mrs. Clough invited the group over to their WHO compound for refreshments, which included glasses of the Clough home-brewed wine. After one glass, Elizabeth made her excuses to Chuck Toiler, Amy and Jessie and left this party with David.

Not wanting to mix homemade wine with hard liquor offered by David, Elizabeth asked for tea or coffee. David countered with Pepsi.

Their tryst progressed in the usual way except this time Elizabeth skipped the illegal American liquor prelude before going to the bedroom with David to make love. She was very grateful that David would always have the trusted American condoms since he had access to almost anything he, as an American Army consultant, wanted whether or not it was forbidden in the Kingdom. And all birth control was forbidden in the Kingdom. Had Elizabeth wanted to start using birth control pills again, she would have had to have a friend in California send them to her with the risk that someone at customs would open the package and keep them. Theft from incoming packages was fairly common. It wouldn't be confiscating them because of their forbidden categorization, but rather, to give to one of the wives of the custom's inspector.

After love making, the two plotters discussed how to find out more about 'Cologne Man.'

"Hamza told me as much about 'Cologne Man' as he

knew," recounted David. "Apparently his father is General Badawy who has six sons and one daughter. 'Cologne Man's' first name is Jamal. Jamal is the sixth son, the baby of the family. All the boys but one went into the National Guard. His father knew he was the spoiled youngest son, kind of a softy, and so he pulled strings to get him assigned to a desk job. But lately, Jamal has been getting hassled. His father suspects he might be homosexual and wants to protect him anyway. Since most of his brothers are also in the Guard, they support their father in this protection. But they know they can't do that forever and would probably welcome a convenient marriage to protect him."

"But would they let him leave the country?" asked Elizabeth.

"I don't know about that but the Badawys are in close to the royal family. If General Badawy wants something, he usually gets it according to Hamza."

"But how would this work? Would Hamza give Amina's telephone number to Jamal and tell him she might be a possible wife that wouldn't be bothered by his homosexuality?" questioned Elizabeth. "Could we manage to get this to happen?" Elizabeth was skeptical that a Saudi would welcome this kind of interference from Americans. She sensed even after less than a year that most Saudis had contempt for most Americans even while they exploited them or traveled to the US to enjoy freedom there.

~~~

Jamal Badawy had only come to recognize how different he was from his brothers when he was a teenage. As a child, he was raised like any other Saudi boy. He played as other
~~~

boys did but had also enjoyed the occasional play with his sister's dolls. His mother and sisters and aunties had thought it was cute so they indulged him without restraint. Since sex education in Saudi Arabia is forbidden, trusting that Allah puts all the proper instincts into each human and expects parents and family to participate in his plan of training binary humanity for family life, despite having five older brothers, Jamal accepted his difference until his hormones kicked in. When his mother caught him trying to wear his sister's *abaya* and *niqab*, she abruptly put a stop to it. He adapted to her negative injunction. He gradually found he very much enjoyed the rough and tumble play of the prepubescent boys at the Islamic school. However, as they got older and the other boys began to discuss their fantasies and desires, he was lost. While he enjoyed the furtive group masturbation sessions in the *wadi* palm grove, he did not understand why the other boys reacted so differently from himself.

~~~

David and Elizabeth made their plans. David would make it his business to get to know Jamal so as to determine whether he might welcome a marriage of protection. Elizabeth promised to confirm with Amina that she would be willing to marry someone who would probably not desire her sexually and needed the protection of heterosexual marriage.

What David learned was that only one of Jamal's brothers was not married. The younger two of the six brothers were not yet married. Jamal had followed his father and brother into the National Guard skipping university. But Ali, his next older brother had avoided the Guard by taking a steward job with Saudia Airlines. The men's parents had
~~~

been talking to families for these two youngest sons to try to find good Saudi wives for them. However, neither of the two youngest sons showed the eagerness their parents thought appropriate to get married. The search continued as Jamal and his brother Ali avoided being available to attend these two family approval and negotiating sessions. The parents were confused and frustrated as each time they brought the subject up, the two youngest sons had arranged to be traveling and often out of the country for example, to Sri Lanka's Kluckman Resort owned by a German, which catered to homosexual men, which was a place to meet or a place to retreat. Ali usually could protest that his job would not allow him to attend marriage negotiating meetings but Jamal had no such excuse as his father would easily discover if he used his office job as an excuse. He felt somewhat protected as he knew that his parents would try to follow the Saudi tradition of older sons being married before younger sons. As long as Ali was not married Jamal felt his parents would not put too much pressure on him. While Jamal was sometimes posted with his group to different bases in the Kingdom, most of his work was near Riyadh. The parents assumed that if the brothers were together, they were OK. Since homosexuality was so prohibited in Saudi Arabia; it did not occur to them that their sons could be so afflicted. General Badawy of course, had been part of decisions to eject homosexual men from the Guard but his conscious mind would not allow him to consider that designation for his Jamal despite Jamal's 'softness.'

David Nelson was able to learn through Hamza that Jamal might welcome a telephone meeting with Amina. Hamza had taken an opportunity while they we riding in the same vehicle to a required training session, that Jamal might be interested in protecting himself from 'normal'

Saudi marriage by participating in a wedding with someone who wished only for a legal male guardian.

David also discovered that Hamza's humanitarian attitude toward a fellow Guardsman came from assisting his own younger brother to escape to the USA for graduate school to avoid exposure of his homosexuality. Hamza was married and had several children himself but he also had enlightened attitudes as were seldom found among Saudi men, often only those exposed to Western ideas by associating with colleagues like David. Hamza's brother had so enjoyed the freedom in America that he had managed to stay after finding a job with another airline in Los Angeles.

Elizabeth and Amina arranged a coded telephone message in order to meet outside the University campus. Since they were already known at the Riyadh Palace Hotel, it was a natural place to them to meet. Their message code was for either one to say to the other, "The Princess wants to meet us at four today." That would be the signal to take a taxi to the café in the Riyadh Palace Hotel. If either could not make that meeting, they would so indicate and then the initiator of the code would say, "I will consult with the Princess."

Amina confirmed to Elizabeth her desire to go forward with an asexual marriage in order to save her life. Elizabeth gave Amina's telephone number to David. They both knew that is would be safer if Jamal called Amina and arranged an assignation in the canned vegetable aisle of the grocery store.

The risk was equal for both of them. Jamal took the risk first and called and reached Mrs. Khoury and left his telephone number to give to Amina. Mrs. Khoury was both excited and scared for her daughter for being contacted by a man. Jamal left no message besides his telephone number which left some mystery. Mrs. Khoury, having four other daughters, had learned some of the newer ways in which girls learned about potential husbands and did not tell her husband who would have thought that he should have been contacted first.

Amina used a pay telephone in the university campus to arrange the first meeting. They did not immediately reject each other. Subsequently, after class, she gave the guard at the University guard shed Jamal's telephone number to call for her ride saying he was her brother. The guard took her at her word as she had always been compliant before. They began to meet this way regularly. They would drive around Riyadh in his requisitioned grey-green National Guard vehicle with the National Guard logo painted on the door for an hour or so with Amina seated in the back seat. Their conversations took place in this more or less protected environment. Then he would drop her off around the corner from her family's villa walls. Eventually, they made their pragmatic decisions to inform their families to arrange the two family pre-engagement meeting.

Elizabeth helped Amina begin to write to US graduate school nursing programs for their catalogues. She would have her senior year at National Saudia University for Girls in which to prepare. Jamal began to think about what US university or college training he might be able to get the National Guard to pay for. Hamza arranged for Jamal and David to begin become acquainted so David could assist him to look at college programs in the USA.

Chapter 26

Destinations

Summer home visit time approached. The spring semester finished with Final Exams. Elizabeth saw it as an opportunity to visit graduate programs while she was home in Los Angeles area. There were so many colleges and universities there. Undoubtedly one of them was probably more supportive of Arabic nursing students like Amina. She planned to discover which it might be.

Elizabeth also decided she would see her gynecologist in Los Angeles and get a diaphragm just in case David ran out of condoms. She could wear it in so if her luggage was inspected for contraband, there would be nothing illegal there.

Meanwhile, with classes over, Amina and Jamal met less frequently but they had worked out ways to communicate with each other while their families negotiated and planned the first meeting. Jamal had Hamza speak to his father about the family of Amina Khoury and begin to start 'getting to know them' and the formal engagement and marriage process.

Two weeks before Elizabeth's departure for the United States home visit, June 13, 1982, King Khalid died which threw the Kingdom temporarily into chaos. National Guard soldiers were visible about every 100 yards along the main streets at Elizabeth took the bus to the University. She discovered to her dismay that Saudi police had come into the campus of National Saudia University for Girls and arrested about forty teachers. Later it was discovered that the arrested faculty were *Shia*, the branch of Islam which has many believing members in Iran, Syria and Turkey. Saudi *Sunnis* had long been paranoid about the intentions of the *Shia* who lived mostly in the Eastern provinces of Saudi Arabia. Apparently this mass arrest was a preventive measure. The Saudi Royal family feared a *Shia* revolution after what had happened in Iran. This made quite a dent in the women's faculty as approximately forty *Shia* women were arrested and taken away and jailed. This set all other faculty on edge, *Sunni* or foreign faculty of which there ware quite a few. The American women faculty were all eager to head for their home visits until things cooled down. It was also good to avoid the most extreme desert temperatures.

Before leaving for Los Angeles, Elizabeth discovered from a catalogue in the library at the National Saudia University for Girls that the University of California at Los Angeles Master of Nursing program which was started in 1966, was friendly toward students from the Middle East. Amina would probably have to take a remedial English class before she could be admitted to the nursing program. But in her precarious situation, Amina did not care how long she stayed away from the Kingdom, or so she thought until she experienced the homesickness with sneaks in for most expatriates after about three months absence from their home culture. But nurses were now valued enough in Saudi Arabia that the government was glad to pay all her expenses; out of state tuition, off campus housing for she and Jamal, as well as all travel to and from the Kingdom. With a masters from the famous UCLA program she could be faculty in any of the new nursing programs opening in different Saudi universities.

David planned to ask Hamza if his brother Ali might be able to help Jamal find a part-job in Los Angeles though he would not need to work if he were enrolled in college as the Saudi government would cover all costs. If he were not accepted at a college, a job would be a back-up. Most consulates and embassies had military attachés. Maybe Jamal could get one of those. Certainly General Badawy could make such a transfer happen.

For her home holiday, Elizabeth made several trips to the *souq* to purchase Saudi mementos for friends in Los Angeles. She bought some of the gaudy brocades with gold threads, brass camel ash trays, several small twelve-inch by twelve-inch handmade fringed carpets. These were not made by Saudis. Saudi carpets, which were rare, were much more crudely made. However, the finer carpets from Iraq, Afghanistan or India were imported to Riyadh in great abundance. She knew most people in Los Angeles could not tell the difference. Her bags were bulging with such gifts. She wore the gold bangle she bought for her sister as she knew it would take her over the customs upper import limit, but if she wore it, she hoped it would miss the custom agent's eyes. She felt it was her right to avoid the custom as Patsy Elgin's absconding and leaving her with paying the bond had short changed the amount she might have spent on gifts for the home folks. Also, she realized this was convoluted reasoning. She hardly packed any clothes as the skirts and dresses she wore in Riyadh would not be good for the casual California life she hoped to sample again at home in Los Angles.

Elizabeth said good bye to David Nelson who took her to the Riyadh Airport, writing his address in her private address book intending to write to him during the home holiday. However, she knew she would soon see Graham Brown and felt a tiny bit of guilt knowing that they would probably resume their old affair. In fact Graham had invited her to spend as much of her holiday in his apartment a she could. She flew from Riyadh to Paris, Paris to Atlanta and Atlanta to Los Angeles International Airport. Graham picked her up. She spent the first night with him. His apartment was like a library. Almost all the walls were covered floor to ceiling with built-in bookshelves. They were all full. There were a few open spots on the walls where hung quality watercolors. For Elizabeth, the familiarity of his condo was reassuring. They drank California red wine while he cooked a dinner of pork roast, gravy, green beans and baked potatoes. Graham expected she might be ready for pork after a year in a country that forbade it. Neither Graham nor Elizabeth spoke about relationships they had had while apart from each other. For Elizabeth it took some managing of her conversations as David had been so involved with the most important events of her time away in Saudi.

Graham was a much more accomplished lover than David, the Army man. But David was more thoughtful and considerate. She tried to NOT compare them but it was hard to ignore their differences in intimate situations.

Elizabeth had stored her car in her sister's garage along with the contents of her bungalow which had been rented to someone else for the duration. Her sister, 'a jewelry hound' was delighted with the gold bangle on which Elizabeth had avoided paying customs. She felt only a little guilt.

When Elizabeth called at the UCLA Nursing Department office, she was shocked to see on a bulletin board in pictures of graduate students and their projects, a photo of Patsy Elgin, the nurse who had not returned from her holiday and left Elizabeth and Aisha, the other nursing faculty at National Saudia University for Girls, with her debt of two months salary bond. The photo showed Patsy standing with a group of children in front of an East Los Angeles clinic. Now this was Elizabeth's dilemma. Should she find someone with clout to tell about this woman and her debt? Or should she try to find the woman herself and confront her?

Chapter 27

Patsy Elgin

Elizabeth was furious to know that the woman who had essentially stolen a month's salary from her was a graduate student at UCLA. Someone like her should not be trusted near patients or their belongings, she felt. That unprofessional behavior of theft should prohibit her from having a professional license, Elizabeth fumed. If she didn't do something about it, it would eat away at her. She stood for a moment immobilized by her anger before she realized that the secretary behind the desk was looking at her expectantly.

She stepped forward and introduced herself, "I am Elizabeth Adams, a nursing instructor in the nursing program at National Saudia Women's University Administration in Riyadh, Saudi Arabia. I have a student who wants to come to graduate school in the states after she graduates this coming year. I wonder if I could get a catalogue of your master of nursing program. Also, do you have many Arab students?"

The secretary turned around on her office chair and examined the bookcase behind her against the wall. She selected the proper catalogue and handed it to Elizabeth as she asked, "Would you like to talk to Dr. Ribon the head of that program?"

"Is she in? Oh, yes if that's possible." Elizabeth could hardly believe her good fortune as often faculty members were not in their offices during summer semester.

The secretary picked up the telephone and punched a button which Elizabeth could hear ringing in a nearby office. A moment later, the office door opened and a short, very professional looking woman with a short curly grey haircut and matching grey pantsuit and silver earrings came out extending her hand toward Elizabeth. "Come in, Miss ___?"

Again Elizabeth introduced herself, "I am Elizabeth Adams, a nursing instructor in the nursing program at National Saudia Women's University Administration in Riyadh, Saudi Arabia. I have a student who wants to come to graduate school in the states after she graduates from our baccalaureate program this coming year. I am trying to help her find the appropriate program."

The grey haired woman gestured toward the chair across the desk from herself. "We have had an Arabic student before but I think she was from Jordan. We helped her adapt her course work to fit what she planned to do when she went home. I see that Linda gave you a catalogue. We are rewriting that catalogue because we have added some classes and cancelled others. If you leave your address in Riyadh, I'll send you a new catalogue when it's published. What other questions do you have?"Meanwhile, Dr. Ribon was thinking how lucrative it was to have these foreign students paying graduate out of state tuition.

Elizabeth considered whether or not she should ask

about the photo of Patsy Elgin. At least she could inquire. "Dr. Ribon, on the bulletin board in the outer office I saw the photo of someone I knew in Saudi Arabia. Her name is Patsy Elgin. I take it she is a student here?"

"Why yes, she is in her first year in our masters program. How did you know her?" questioned Dr. Ribon.

Elizabeth had not suspected that Patsy had had only a baccalaureate in nursing, not a master's as most National Saudia Women's University faculty did. Now Elizabeth was forced to consider whether to tell Dr. Ribon half the truth or the whole thing about Patsy's betrayal of her colleagues. While thieves in Saudi Arabia still had their thieving right hand surgically removed, they did not chop off hands anymore. But the National Saudia Women's University Administration would probably think there was no crime since the two colleagues had freely signed Patsy's papers. Besides, the Dean had already shown his disregard for the betrayal by Patsy Elgin.

Elizabeth decided to start out with the half truth, "She was on the faculty of Nursing at National Saudia Women's University when I arrived to teach there. She taught the infectious disease nursing."

Elizabeth did not go on to explain yet, that Patsy had left others to finish teaching that class. She waited for Dr. Ribon's response.

Chapter 28

Amina and Jamal

Amina got over her initial distaste for the idea of being married to someone who did not sexually desire her, someone who would probably not father children with her. The alternative was not good. Her sympathy for his situation grew as they spent time alone together discussing their dilemmas. She did not come 'all out' with her story immediately until she had learned to trust him. Eventually she confessed the grievous breech of Saudi sexual standards that she had committed with Dr. Maloof and its consequence. It took her even longer to describe to Jamal the role of her teacher in trying to solve her problem. With such a price to be paid by each of them, teacher and student, if the truth were discovered, Amina was slow in disclosing her story. This was still happening at the same time as Elizabeth scouted MSN programs in Southern California.

Jamal also took time to disclose the story of his life in his family of brothers whom he worshipped if Muslims can worship anything except Allah, but, brothers that he could not emulate. He told how his father had facilitated his induction into the Saudi National Guard and his subsequently being assigned to the desk job in the quartermaster corp. He recounted his first recognition of his sexual desire differences and his attempts to conceal it. He was not graphic in describing his first real sexual encounters, simply telling her of his own emotions with his first love, a Bahraini policeman who had come to Riyadh for training.

Part of Jamal's job was to arrange for the housing and feeding of the trainees. Jamal had rented a vacant villa outside Riyadh where he had had installed cots for the trainees as well as cooks for the meals which were served in the courtyard. Most of the training was done on the field nearby except for the Western police training movies with Arabic sub-titles which were shown in the parlor of the villa where the trainees sat on the carpets Jamal had purchased in the souq. The *hookahs* and stories had come out at night after the movies and before the final prayer time. He and the Bahraini trainee's eyes had met several times during the sessions which Jamal had to attend in order to make sure all the trainees and instructors needs were fulfilled. During a movie he sat down beside the Bahraini man and eventually they agreed to skip prayer time and meet outside the walls. Jamal rolled up one of the carpets and unrolled it at the far edge of the dusty field of parked cars under an acacia tree. The Bahraini man, who had fewer restrictions than Saudi men, was somewhat experienced and initiated the delights which Jamal had never before experienced, only dreamt about. It was the Bahraini man who reminded Jamal that his name meant 'Beauty.'

Jamal alluded to this first experience only in poetic terms in describing it for Amina. Being a feeling and warm hearted young woman, Amina could relate to his reticence in sharing his story as she had experienced somewhat the same emotions with Dr. Maloof during their drives through Riyadh to the desert. She was not explicit in her description of her experience either. Both used poetic terms to refer to their first loves. After all, many Arabs thought Arabic was the epitome of poetic language. There were many love songs and ballads in Arabic.

Eventually, they confessed to each other the brotherly and sisterly feelings that were developing between them. They agreed that living together as brother and sister under the camouflage of marriage was a better alternative to beheading, or the simple shooting as the Princess in "Death of a Princess" experienced.

By the time the two families met, Amina and Jamal were comfortable with their own plans and felt they could comply with whatever their families arranged in the marriage contract. Since public affection is discouraged and even forbidden in Saudi Arabia except for the obligatory three kiss greetings between people of the same sex, they were not forced to feign physical affection.At the end of the evening, they were considered properly engaged. Wedding plans began.

~~~

David Nelson had picked Elizabeth up at the airport and driven her to the University Hospital flats when she returned from holiday. It was somewhat of an emotional adjustment to see him again after eight weeks of frequent intimacy with Graham Brown. But her jet related fatigue plus class preparations for the new junior class which had five new students and the preparation for attending the wedding kept her from having to spend time with David. She was glad of it though she anticipated returning to such intimacy, she needed a few more days to adjust to the idea
~~~

of her relationship with him. While she felt little guilt by now about two relationships, she needed time between to adapt her emotions in responding to two different men.

When Elizabeth returned from Los Angeles, she was just in time to attend the wedding. The couple and their families had fixed the wedding date two weeks before classes started for Amina's senior year so the couple could have a honeymoon in Bahrain, Saudi Arabia's playground. Elizabeth was somewhat still jet-lagged as the wedding was four days after her return to Riyadh. However, with the ingestion of sufficient Arabic coffee, she was able to seem lively as an honored guest.

Because she had so little time to prepare as she only learned the wedding date upon her arrival back at National Saudia University for Girls, she went to the tailor's booth in the women's souq and ordered a special dress for Amina's wedding. It was brown lace over peach colored taffeta. Her twenty-four carat gold English half-crown earrings complimented her coloring and the gold thread in the brown lace. It also complimented Elizabeth's red brown hair and pale peach colored skin. This dress was splurging for Elizabeth who was used to sewing her own clothes, but she knew in her jetlagged condition she would not be able to quickly sew such challenging fabrics. The dress was ready with the final fitting the morning of the wedding. As she donned her clothes to join Amy and Jessie who were also invited to the wedding, she thought what a shame it was to cover her lovely new gown with the black *abaya*. But her matching peach colored sandals showed beneath it. The three women took a cab together to the wedding.

While driving together to the wedding villa, Jessie reported that the Committee for the Promotion of Virtue and the

Prevention of Vice had discovered that RICF was meeting in the Lockheed Compound and forced the cessation of the Friday meetings. The minister and his wife had been deported within twenty-four hours of the discovery. Apparently, some local authorities had always been aware of these meetings and ignored the fact that these Christians were breaking Saudi law. A spy, pretending to be a Coptic Christian from Egypt, had consistently attended meetings and kept the local authorities informed. The prince who had allowed these meetings had somehow offended another prince who reported them to the Committee for the Promotion of Virtue and the Prevention of Vice and they had pounced. The Christian community in Riyadh was very upset by this development as they had to go underground without their pastor. A few folks continued to meet nervously in each other's flats and villas.

~~~

The women's wedding party took place in a villa especially built for such events. The taxi dropped them off at the elaborate wrought iron gate in the twelve-foot high walled compound. As Amina's teachers, they were given an honored place on the front row with the mothers of the bride and groom and Amina's Aunt Maymunah. Sister Fatimah was largely pregnant and sat in the front row, too. Her classmates and their mothers sat in the second row. Elizabeth turned to them as Fairuz and Mouna each gave her the three kiss greeting.

The room glittered with gold finery as well as brocades, laces and silk *peau de soie* gowns. Many of the women had special *henna* designs on their hands and forearms. The women all kept their face veils handy for when the groom and his father were expected. The black women servers
~~~

were carrying trays of small cups of the famous Arabic coffee. Another server carried a *Dallah*, the Arabic coffee pot, and refilled the small cups. Baskets of sweets were also presented to guests. The musicians were a different women's band than the one that had played at her sister Fatimah's wedding. No males entered the room as they had at Fatimah's wedding to bring more chairs or do other errands, until after the procession of the small cousins and younger sister would-be brides carrying the dangerous long tapers. Fatimah had offered her wedding dress to Amina but Amina wanted her own style. Amina, dressed in an ivory *peau de soie* ball gown type wedding dress, enhanced with ivory Belgian lace around the plunging neckline and cascading down to the hem, came in with Jamal, who was dressed in a gold embroidered *thobe*. They came together up unto the stage and each sat in one of the throne like carved chairs.

A procession of female relatives came to give gold jewelry to Amina. Then Jamal opened a large jewelry case he had been balancing on his knee and shook the gold bib to make all the links straighten out before going behind Amina's chair and fixing the clasp at the back. Then, after a few minutes, they arose as a couple and led the women into the feast in the room next door. After about fifteen minutes, they waved to the guests still gorging themselves on fresh fruit, kebobs, spiced boiled eggs, and pastries, and departed to drive to the East Coast of Saudi Arabia to take a ferry boat to Bahrain. They left their car at the ferry boat parking lot. The building of the new causeway which was much discussed in the *Arab News* had not yet been started.

They were so tired by the time they arrived, that they immediately went to sleep in the two different beds in their hotel suite. The first full day after they arrived, they spent exploring the Island, Amina with her face uncovered as a sort of rebellion against Saudi rules for women to keep their faces covered. That night after dinner, Jamal did drink a cocktail which Amina refused because too much rebellion at once was not her style. Besides, she had plans to try to see if she could seduce him despite his declared homosexuality. She needed her wits. Her knowledge of homosexuality was meager at best. In the same way many straight men think they could probably, with their spectacular lovemaking, make a lesbian into a straight woman, Amina hoped she might be able to convince Jamal that he desired her. Jamal tried but his body would not respond so eventually, he apologized and they returned to their two different beds and finally fell asleep apart.

The next night, Jamal had a few drinks sent up to the room before they tried again. After another failure to get an erection, they again went to the two different beds in the suite. As soon as Jamal felt that Amina was fully asleep, he slipped out of the suite. Amina was not asleep and immediately sat up crying, imagining where Jamal was going. Jamal found the pay phone in the lobby where he called his first love, the Bahraini Imad, whose telephone number he had kept all these months.

He could hear Western music and voices in the background when eventually, Imad picked up the receiver. "Allo, allo?"

Jamal looked around him to make sure nobody was within listening distance before he said in Arabic, "Imad, its Jamal Badawy from Riyadh. I'm here in Manama."

"Well come on over. As you can hear, we're having a

party," the slurred voice of Imad replied. "Let me give you the address."

Jamal's drinks had by now worn off with the effort to envision Imad while trying to get an erection with Amina. "Oh, I'm sorry. I'd rather see you alone. Can we get together tomorrow?"

"Call me tomorrow." Imad hung up.

The next day, Jamal and Amina walked to the beach. Though it was possible for women to swim here on Manama beach, Amina was too shy, having never had the opportunity to experience the joy of water immersion. They watched the others in the water and playing on the beach. Women were all completely covered except for their faces but small children, both boys and girls frolicked in the water with their fathers. However, some women waded in the water with their skirts and *abayas* pulled up to keep them out of the water.

"If you don't mind, tonight I'd like to visit with an old Bahraini friend who lived in Manama. Would that bother you?" questioned Jamal in Arabic.

"Jamal, I am so sorry I haven't been able to arouse you. I hope someday I can so I can get pregnant but, yes, go visit you friend," Amina replied with real sadness.

Jamal kept his promise of acting like a husband whenever he was with Amina, except for sexual intercourse. He rubbed her back, brought her food, and encouraged her to explore the *souqs* of Manama. Except for the disappointment about being unable to change Jamal to a heterosexual, Amina enjoyed the honeymoon.

When the couple returned from Bahrain, they moved into General Badawy's compound. They were given their own small villa where Amina was in charge of the household functions. She was friendly with Jamal's other family members. Jamal drove her to her classes before going on the National Guard compound.

When classes resumed, Amina, as in the past, made excuses to stay after class to talk to Elizabeth. Her English was getting much better. During this time, Amina told Elizabeth about her failure to change her husband's desire but their otherwise pleasant honeymoon. There were so many things to discuss; UCLA, job or graduate program in Southern California for both Amina and Jamal, and possibly artificial insemination. This was a completely new concept for Amina, so Elizabeth gave her a description how that could happen. It would be easy if they did it in California.

Chapter 29

Patsy Elgin Again

In the envelope with the new UCLA Nursing Masters curriculum description, there was a typed letter on thick UCLA letterhead paper from Dr. Ribon:

Dear Ms. Adams,   October 29, 1982

During your visit here in July, when we discussed the possibility of one of your Saudi Arabian students applying for this program, I had the feeling that there was something more about Patsy Elgin that you were holding back. I did not want to press you at that time. But since then, she has applied for a teaching assistant position here which would be to teach beginning nursing classes in the undergraduate program. Consequently, I thought I'd ask again if you had any additional information for me. Your reply will be kept absolutely confidential.

Also if you have further questions related to your Arab student, do not hesitate to inquire.

Yours,

Christine Ribon

Dr. Christine Ribon

Director of the Masters in Nursing Program

University of California at Los Angeles

Elizabeth took several days to consider whether and how much she should tell Dr. Ribon. Would she sound petty if she told Dr. Ribon that Patsy Elgin owed her money? Or was it a professional obligation to expose such untrustworthiness. These were the same arguments, indeed the same dialogues she had had with herself ever since she realized she was obligated to pay National Saudia University for Girls a month's salary approximately $1800 or about $5500 riyals.

Eventually, she decided to report, as professionally as possible, the exact truth as she knew it. She asked Amal if she could use the typewriter. Elizabeth waited that afternoon until everyone had left the department before sitting down at Amal's typewriter.She decided to use a regular plain paper and envelope rather than the National Saudia University for Girls letterhead since she knew that the Dean's office male secretary photocopied all outgoing mail envelopes. She determined to take it to the main post office herself.

Dr. Christine Ribon

Director of the Masters in Nursing Program

University of California at Los Angeles
November 15, 1982

Thank you for sending the updated nursing masters catalogue for our Saudi Arabian student. I brought back the application form which I got from your secretary that day in July. This student Amina Khoury has since gotten married but in Saudi Arabia, women do not necessarily take their husband's name so she will be applying in her own name.

In your letter you inquired if I knew anything further about Patsy Elgin whom you are considering for a teaching assistantship. I did withhold some important information while talking to you in your office. I was and am reluctant to say anything negative about someone in our profession; however, after considering the matter carefully, I think it is proper for me to tell you what I know.

When I arrived in Riyadh, Miss Elgin was teaching the communicable disease sections of the curriculum while I have been teaching the basic medical surgical units. It is a policy of National Saudia University for Girls to require expatriate faculty who wish to leave the Kingdom for a holiday or before their contract is finished, to post two months of salary as a bond to assure that person's return as some expatriate faculty may become homesick and leave early. One alternative for the faculty member is to get two colleagues to sign documents promising to pay the two months salary bond if the person who has traveled doesn't return to finish their contract. Patsy Elgin persuaded me and another faculty member to sign such a document so that she could travel during the pilgrimage vacation last fall. When she did not return, we each forfeited a month's salary as we had promised. She made no attempt to contact or compensate us. You can be sure; we were very angry and disappointed with her. Additionally, we had to decide who would take up the obligation of teaching her classes. You can see from this story why I was reluctant to share this information with you. You must do as you see fit related to this matter which I consider theft.

I hope this will not impact the application of Amina Khoury. She is an exemplary student.

Yours sincerely,

Elizabeth Adams MSN RN

National Saudia University for Girls

Riyadh, Saudi Arabia

She took the bus to the main post office, bought an overseas stamp and mailed the letter. It took approximately two weeks to travel from Riyadh to Los Angeles.

The next day after class, she sat with Amina and helped her fill out the application. This took them several sessions with rewriting the required essay about her reasons for wanting a master's degree and making a list of English speaking faculty who would recommend her. Jessie and Amy, as well as Samia agreed to write recommendations for her. It was late December when she mailed it from the National Saudia University for Girls Nursing Department. By now Amina had shared her intention with her classmates. They attributed her previous sessions with Elizabeth after class to this ambition, to them, a permissible goal.

Elizabeth did not receive a reply to her letter until after Christmas. Dr. Ribon thanked her for completing the story about Patsy Elgin without saying what she did with the information. Additionally, she said she looked forward to receiving Amina Khoury's application. She included a brochure which apparently went to all graduate school applicants showing community housing information as well as resources available on campus.

The spring semester was uneventful for the three students, Amina, Fairuz, and Mouna. They all three achieved an acceptable level of nursing skill and knowledge so that they could pass a nursing exam in the USA should they try to do that. Amina would need to do that on the UCLA campus before being able to enroll in any of the masters level classes.

Amina received her acceptance letter to the UCLA Masters of Nursing Program in early May. She held a celebration party in her mother-in-law's villa. While Amina did not have a women's band, she had a wonderful selection of recorded music by Middle Easterners. The women danced with each other. If their dresses did not allow their hip movements to show sufficiently, there were long scarves to tie around the hips so the sensuality of Saudi dancing could be seen and experienced. Girls danced with girl partners in a similar fashion to male-female dancing in the USA, facing each other, dancing separately, but mirroring each other's movements.

The late June ceremony for graduates from every department at National Saudia University for Girls was held in the girls' gymnasium. Sections of the bleachers near the playing floor were reserved for a hundred or so students and nearly that many royal princesses who had been invited to attend. The clothing and jewelry was equally as dazzling as Elizabeth had seen at weddings. There were no men there. No fathers saw their daughters achieve this success. The royal princesses processed in following the procession of faculty and then the students who were seated chairs on the gymnasium floor. Several female heads of divisions as well as one of the princesses gave short speeches in Arabic. The program was all printed in Arabic and despite her continued study of the Arabic language, Elizabeth had difficulty following everything. She was able to find her students' names in the list. Even this level of understanding of Arabic language felt like a triumph!

Mouna invited her classmates and their female family members, and the nursing faculty to her family's villa for a graduation celebration. It followed the similar female party pattern. First came the tiny cups of coffee and tea, followed by trays of special chocolates and small pastries. Recorded Middle Eastern music played in the background. Eventually the hostess arose and chose Fairuz to dance with her and signaled to Amina to choose one of the faculty to dance. Amina, of course, chose Elizabeth, grabbing scarves to tie around their hips. Elizabeth did her best to mimic Amina more sensual movements. The women in the room *ululated*, a vocalization by fast tongue movement, and clapped even more loudly in appreciation for this foreign teacher's efforts.

Chapter 30

Acceptance

Jamal had not gone to college or university before he went straight into the Saudi National Guard from high school, so he applied to several undergraduate programs in the Los Angeles area and was accepted at Occidental College near Pasadena. That Liberal Arts Campus had accepted foreign students for many years where most had thrived. Elizabeth had been able to assure him that he would be comfortable studying there as there were many other foreign students. She knew how hard it was to speak a foreign language constantly rather than native language. She was sure he would find other Arab speakers there with whom he could study.

Amina had received her acceptance letter into the UCLA Masters in Nursing Program in time to make a round of goodbye visits to family and friends before departure with Jamal; however her National Saudia University for Girls teachers were all on holiday away from Riyadh. Amina had promised Elizabeth that she would write regularly. Additionally, Elizabeth gave Amina David Nelson's mailing address just in case there was anything sensitive enough that she did not want the Dean's office to perhaps open and photocopy. Neither Elizabeth nor Amina completely trusted the Dean's office not to open it if it looked interesting or offensive.

In the Saudi flight from Riyadh to Jeddah and from Jeddah to Rome, the women were boarded first and sent to the front to the first class section and the men went into the business class section. It was not until they boarded the Pan American flight from Rome to Atlanta that they were seated together. While Amina had thrown her face veil off as soon as they left the Jeddah Airport, it was not until she walked through the airport in Rome without her veil that she first felt the nakedness of an uncovered face. Both by then were able to breathe sighs of relief to be away from the country of their birth where they could both be severely punished. By then there were no other Arab speakers around, so they were able to commiserate together about their nervousness about the adventure ahead. Eventually they slept and awoke in time to change planes in Atlanta Hartsfield Airport for the Los Angeles International Airport.

Elizabeth on holiday home leave, had recovered her car from her sister's garage when she first arrived, so she was able to meet them at LAX as they came through customs and drive them to a hotel near the UCLA campus. Knowing how bewildering Los Angeles could be for newcomers, she promised to meet them again in the morning and take them to the campus for Amina to begin the necessary paperwork for enrollment. First thing the next morning Elizabeth took them to the motel café where she spread out a map of Los Angeles.

Since Amina had never learned to drive, the couple looked at the map of where their university and college were geographically situated and decided that they should find an apartment in Santa Monica or West Hollywood so she could walk to campus. Or at least be close enough to take the bus or for Jamal to take her to class before he drove on through Los Angeles to Occidental College in Eagle Rock. Jamal felt that a first order of business after finding an apartment would be to buy a car.

They did not arise until late morning the next day before telephoning Elizabeth who spent her next day driving them around looking for FOR RENT signs within that area. Jamal remarked, "Strange, woman driving me."

Money was no limitation as the Saudi government subsidized all their college and university students studying overseas. Eventually they settled for a furnished two bedroom apartment in a complex near Wilshire Boulevard with an assigned parking place. Next on the agenda was perusing the automobile sale lots. Jamal was used to the new Chevy Caprice his parents had given him on his twenty first birthday or the National Guard vehicles. They had promised him that the car he would buy in America would be a wedding present. He settled on a brand new 1982 silver Chevy Camaro.

A driver's license for Jamal was next though his Saudi license would work for a month or so. But Elizabeth wanted them to be more or less settled before she returned to Riyadh to start the fall semester. She reviewed the rules-of-the-road traffic law book and had Jamal take her for a ride the next afternoon.She guessed that his stint in the National Guard had taught him more about proper driving than anything he could have learned from the chaos of Riyadh traffic. Certainly, Los Angeles traffic was less lethal than Riyadh's. Amina, having never driven nor contemplated the skill required, was glad to have Jamal and Elizabeth pursue this adventure without her while she walked Wilshire Boulevard looking in the shops.

Having settled the transportation issues for the young couple, Elizabeth went with Amina to enroll in classes. She knew Amina's strengths and weakness and made sure she enrolled in a medical terminology class as well as a remedial English class the first semester. Because cost was of little concern to the Saudi government which was paying for all her expenses, if she took longer to finish her graduate program, there would be no penalty.Amina and Elizabeth took some time to arrange how they would use the US and Saudi mail to communicate, including code sentences and words.

Amina was getting used to walking around without an *abaya* or even a *hijab* over her hair. She seemed set to put her 'nose to the grindstone' in studying. Meanwhile Jamal enjoyed the cosmopolitan atmosphere of Occidental College compared to life in Saudi Arabia. He was exposed to new foods, new music and the gay bars of Los Angeles. The pair found the best places to eat familiar Middle Eastern foods. With Amina's fairly heavy class load, they most often went their two separate ways. Both enjoyed the freedom of attending movie theaters together on weekends. American movies were forbidden in the Kingdom except on the Aramco compound in Dhahran. Though the Saudis were taking over this American/Saudi oil enterprise, most privileges which had been given to American resident workers were still in force.

Only after she was enrolled in the graduate obstetrics class and began to learn more about artificial insemination, did she start to discuss this possibility with Jamal. Because he was so enjoying his new found freedom, his new friends, he put her off saying, "We'll have plenty of time for that when we finish our degrees."

Amina realized that pregnancy would be a challenge while she was still studying so she had not pressed the point.

One of their greatest adventures was going to Santa Monica Beach. Amina wore a one piece bathing suit under a caftan which she could not be persuaded to remove. Even the experience of looking freely at other beach-goers, seemed quite daring to Amina. Jamal had visited other beaches besides that in Manama, Bahrain, and consequently, felt no guilt in staring. There were women in bikinis, men wearing thongs and Speedos.Amina would glance at the latter and quickly look away before anyone, including Jamal, could realize what she was looking at. Despite having looked in textbooks of naked bodies in nursing classes as well as viewing a few almost nude bodies of patients in the clinics and the hospital, a live body running on the beach with only the most intimate parts of the body covered was a strain for Amina to look at. The girls with bouncy breasts playing volleyball was a revelation of freedom she had not imagined despite the propaganda she had read about America. She was able to confess this embarrassment to Elizabeth who listened with empathy. Amina and Jamal had reached a stage of acceptance with each living separate lives in separate bedrooms and separate universities with separate schedules. Amina seldom discussed her daily thoughts and endeavors with her 'husband.'

Elizabeth had plenty of time to devote to the couple since her sister worked, and Graham Brown had gone with a group of other teachers to Japan with People to People tours to visit schools and meet with Japanese educators.

Chapter 31

Dealing with Patsy

Dr. Ribon had not notified Elizabeth about what she planned to do with the information about Patsy leaving nursing colleagues with her debt. Elizabeth guessed about what she thought had happened when she saw Patsy Elgin's name on a list of upcoming professional hearings in the back of the *California Journal of Nursing*. While the hearing date with the California Board of Registered Nursing was scheduled for Patsy after Elizabeth's departure for Riyadh for the fall semester, she wondered if she should write testimony to be presented. She had maintained her membership in the California Nurses Association. Since Aisha Al Aben was Egyptian, would they want her testimony, too? Could she persuade Aisha to write something?

Rather than wonder, she decided to call Dr. Ribon who invited her to come into her office rather than to discuss such a sensitive issue on the telephone.

As Elizabeth prepared to leave for her third year teaching in National Saudia University for Girls, she squeezed in an appointment with Dr. Ribon. She felt she needed to call on her tenants to make sure her house was still in good order. They mailed the checks to her bank and so far, there had been no problem with this system. But otherwise, she did not hear from them. She just wanted them to know she was still alive and aware.

It was freshman orientation week when she arrived on UCLA campus and parked her VW in the parking lot. There was hardly any room anywhere. She had to park at the far end of the lot and walk quite a distance in the August heat. Elizabeth reminded herself that August heat would be much worse in Riyadh and she would be wearing an *abaya*.

When she got to the lobby of the Nursing office, students with paperwork filled the waiting area. She made herself known to the secretary and stood as all the seats were taken. She took the opportunity to observe these students in jeans and shorts and wondered how Amina would fit in, but these she supposed were undergraduates and she would be associating with more mature professionals.

When Dr. Ribon appeared and ushered Elizabeth into her office, she seemed frazzled. "I wanted to discuss with you in private about Patsy Elgin. She did finish up her thesis and is ready to defend it. I am not on her committee. However, I discussed your letter with one of the professors on her thesis committee. She reported it to the California Board of Registered Nursing who felt it deserved investigation. They sent her a registered letter to appear. I expect you will already be back in Saudi Arabia by the time of her hearing.

"Yes, indeed I will be back in Riyadh at the National Saudia University for Girls." Elizabeth was actually glad she would not have to attend such a hearing as it would be stressful watching another nurse being questioned and possibly disciplined. She just wanted her money and

Aisha's money back.

"Well, I wonder if you would like me to submit your letter to the Board as evidence?" asked Dr. Ribon.

"You could do that, or I could write out a specific description of what I know and what rules National Saudia University for Girls has about this issue," suggested Elizabeth thinking such a document might carry more weight than a simple letter.

"I think that's a good idea. Irma, my secretary, is a notary public and you could sign it in front of her and she could send it for you. Do you want to do that now or another time?" questioned Dr. Ribon.

"I'd better do it now as I am leaving in three days and won't have time to get back down here. Is there a quiet place I could sit so I can write it carefully? If I sit out there with all the students, I'm afraid I'll get distracted," replied Elizabeth.

"Let me show you're the conference room. I think that's quiet right now," Dr. Ribon said as she rose and led the way. "If you want me to read it before you sign it, I'll be glad to do so. I have a friend on the Board of Registered Nursing and we've discussed their procedures often so I can probably tell you if it's persuasive enough." She handed Elizabeth several sheets of plain paper and departed.

Elizabeth wrote:

TO WHOM IT MAY CONCERN: August 1, 1982

I want to submit this document as evidence to be used in the professional hearing for Patsy Elgin. Miss Elgin was on the faculty of the Nursing program at National Saudia University for Girls, Riyadh, Kingdom of Saudi Arabia when I arrived to teach there in the autumn of 1980. The University has a policy that if an expatriate faculty desires to leave the Kingdom of Saudi Arabia for other than a yearly home holiday, that that employee must pay two months of salary as a bond of assurance that they will return to finish their contract. There is another option, which is to persuade two colleagues to sign a university document promising that they will pay the bond if the traveler fails to return.

In 1980, shortly after my arrival, Miss Elgin persuaded me and Aisha Al Aben, an Egyptian faculty member to sign such a document for her when she went to Pakistan during the annual Pilgrimage holiday. She did not return, causing each of us to forfeit a month's salary as we had agreed to do. Miss Elgin made no attempt to contact or repay us. Nor had she made any preparation for her teaching her class on communicable disease.

Elizabeth took the paper and knocked on Dr. Ribon's door. She was instructed to come in. She handed Dr. Ribon the page she had written.

After reading it, Dr. Ribon looked up and said, "Let me ask Irma to type this before you sign it and she notarizes it." Then she continued, "When are you going to come back and enroll in a doctoral program? You know if you want to stay in university teaching, eventually, you will need a doctorate."

"I know," responded Elizabeth. "But right now, I don't have the money and besides, I am enjoying the adventure of Saudi Arabia despite the stresses."

~~~

Graham Brown returned to Los Angeles two days before Elizabeth was scheduled to return to Riyadh. Elizabeth picked him up in her car and took him to his apartment. They spent the night together but Graham was so jet-lagged that it was an unsatisfactory evening related to sex relations. He made her promise to meet him if she had any opportunity to get to Europe. Saudi Arabia did not have visitor visas, only pilgrimage, business or foreign workers' visas, the *igama*.

As Elizabeth boarded her flight from LAX to Atlanta Hartsfield Airport to return to Riyadh, she wondered what would happen to Patsy; would she lose her nursing license?

By now, her fourth time, she had accepted the customary donning of her *abaya* between Rome and Jeddah. She had carried it home to Los Angeles. After her departure in June when she wore the *abaya* onto the flight departing Riyadh so that she was indistinguishable from the other women
~~~

who sat up in first class, she had repacked the *abaya* into her overnight case where it remained all summer awaiting this return flight. She left her face uncovered when she disembarked at her final destination. Most foreign women left their faces uncovered, while all Saudi women covered their faces whenever there was a chance of being seen by an unrelated male.

David Nelson met Elizabeth after she cleared customs at the Riyadh International Airport. They spoke little until she was seated in the backseat of his car. They were unable to exchange an affectionate hug until he carried her two suitcases past the little 'guard dog' at the entrance to the University Hospital flats and into Elizabeth's own flat. She followed carrying her overnight case looking like any obedient Muslim woman, she thought regretfully.

David informed her that he was being reassigned back to the Pentagon and had only a few more weeks here in Riyadh. Since Ina Brooks was at home in the flat and since the couple had never made love in Elizabeth's flat anyway, they said goodbye with only a few hugs and kisses and promising to get together as soon as Elizabeth's jetlag was over and both their work schedules allowed.

Soon Elizabeth was deep into planning class schedules and lessons. By now, her third year she was an integral trusted part of this diverse faculty of nurses. While new faculty came and went as their life situations changed, the stable leadership of Jessie with the support of Amy made this foreign work situation as pleasant as possible.

Chapter 32

Letters from Amina

The whole nursing faculty was pleased to hear news about Amina and Jamal when Elizabeth received letters. She was their first baccalaureate nursing graduate to go overseas to graduate school. Amal always sought Elizabeth out immediately when a letter arrived, lurking around to hear the news and passing it on, speaking Arabic to faculty more comfortable in that language. Teaching was supposed to be done in English to prepare medical professionals to be able to communicate well with others in their field for whom English was the predominant language world-wide; however, it was not uncommon to hear information being given to students in their native Arabic despite the rule. So far, no one had been chastised for this departure from policy. The English speaking faculty recognized that students often understood lessons taught in their native language better than in English.

None of the other faculty knew that Amina and Jamal had a marriage of convenience and assumed that she would soon be pregnant. Elizabeth was careful to report only the parts of the letters which would not reveal Amina and Jamal's secret. She did not leave the letters in her desk, but rather in her handbag which she took home daily. Had she allowed the facts about their situation out among the faculty, it could eventually get back to their families making it dangerous and impossible for them to return home for visits.

In December, Elizabeth received a letter:

> *Dear Mrs. Elizabeth,*
>
> *My studies go well. I am getting the grade of "B" in most classes. Some teachers help me and some students have joined a study group to review lectures. This is helpful. I talk by telephone with my sisters and mother on Fridays. I have met a few people from Riyadh which helps me. I remember you told me about 'homesick.' I was homesick in October but I am better now with Saudi friends. Please tell me any news of my classmates.*
>
> *Sincerely,*
>
> *Amina Khoury*

Her written English was obviously getting better. Elizabeth wrote right back to her and included a sheet of paper on which she had asked other faculty members who had taught Amina to write notes to her, too. They now had six students in the new junior class, the biggest class they had had so far.

David Nelson departed promising to write often after he got settled near Washington D.C. He invited her to visit him there next summer on home holiday. They had one last lovely night together before he left. Elizabeth felt slightly bereft for a week or so. She had thought for a time that since his divorce became final, they might have a more permanent relationship.

At the next Desert Ramblers meeting, she met an interesting U.S. Treasury Department consultant to the Saudi Ministry of Finance named Siegfried Meyer who invited her to join him for a Desert Ramblers outing to see some petroglyphs. Sieg was a tall, handsome, slightly slumped man with grey frosting around the edges of his full head of dark hair. She rode in his Buick along with Amy and Jessie. During the outing, he found time alone with Elizabeth to ask for her phone number. She wondered if Amy or Jessie might be jealous since he was more their age than hers, but they seemed pleased when she mentioned to them that she would see him again. While she had considered once or twice that these women might have a homosexual relationship, all their public behavior and conversation seemed to disavow that. She put it out of her mind. Both had been married, had children and divorced, but that did not preclude homosexuality as she had discovered.

Sieg was perhaps the most cosmopolitan man she had ever dated. He had lived around Washington D.C. for most of his adult life. His parents had immigrated to the US from Germany a few years after World War I. He spoke German, as well as passable Arabic and English of course. He continued to invite Elizabeth out to the few performances of music and theater that expatriates were able to cobble together and enjoy under the prohibitions of the Committee for the Promotion of Virtue and the Prevention of Vice.

At his residence which was in a completely separate block of flats, not associated with any government organization as many were, so there was no 'watchdog' at the entrance. The man was a collector of antiques, of relics of archeology, of old coins and books. His flat was crowded with art but organized and could not be considered cluttered. And he was a comfortable person to be with despite having a wife in Washington D.C. from whom he had been separated for many years. That situation made foreign work very attractive to him.

~~~

In March, she received a letter from Amina with the bad news that Jamal was sick and had dropped out of his second semester at Occidental College. She was worried about whether the Saudi government would continue to pay for both of them since he was no longer enrolled. He was spending much of his time in bed sleeping.

Elizabeth immediately replied asking after Jamal's other symptoms. Amina had not described anything specific except that he was not attending classes anymore and was sleeping a lot.

Amina's reply in April was that he had pneumonia and had been briefly hospitalized for it. He also had some peculiar skin lesions that the doctor called Kaposi sarcoma. She briefly mentioned her own classes, but it was obvious
~~~

in the letter that she was very worried about her husband's health. Because of his ill health, they would not be able to return home to Riyadh for the summer vacation.

Elizabeth worked hard to keep up with new discoveries about disease since such patients often ended up on medical-surgical wards especially in places like Riyadh which had so many foreign workers. She remembered reading the article from U.S. Center for Disease Control in *Morbidity and Mortality Weekly Report*, the research about the newly identified disease, human immunodeficiency virus. Elizabeth immediately recalled the symptoms it had described; unexplained weight loss, swollen lymph nodes, fever and rash, and the soft-tissue cancer known as Kaposi's sarcoma. This must be what Jamal had.

Poor Amina! Poor Jamal! There seemed to be no cure for this newly discovered disease. What solace could she provide in letters? She wondered if Amina was aware of the new research. It seemed unlikely that a master's level student in a big university like UCLA could be ignorant of this newly identified disease. Should she share her knowledge with anyone here about this new disease? Did she have an obligation to inquire about whether any of the nursing faculty had come across patients with these symptoms in their hospital or clinic visits here in Riyadh?

CHAPTER 33

SIEG

As they came to know each other, Elizabeth wondered why Sieg, unlike most other westerners, especially the ones in protected prestigious institutions such as the Ministry of Finance, did not brew his own alcoholic beverages, especially since he was living in a block of flats with no 'watch dog.' Eventually, Sieg confessed that he was a 'recovering alcoholic' which made Saudi Arabia, where alcohol is forbidden, the perfect place for him to work. Nonetheless, he had discovered the meeting places and times of several Alcoholics Anonymous groups. On one of their dates, he introduced Elizabeth to another alcoholic from one of the AA groups who accompanied them to look for pottery shards and other artifacts in an old village which had been destroyed by the Muslim Brotherhood in the late 1930s. Most of Sieg's socializing was with other American consultants in the Finance Ministry except with those men he had met in AA. This man was one of those. Unlike meetings in the USA, there were no women in the Riyadh AA meetings. They met in compounds of Western companies such as Lockheed. While the International Christian Fellowship had been instructed to stop having meetings in Lockheed Compound, AA had managed to continue their covert meetings.

Elizabeth had worked with alcoholics in hospital recovery before she settled on the medical surgical specialty. Additionally, she had had the experience of dating an alcoholic engineer during the interim between nursing school and her masters' degree. So she knew that relationships with alcoholics could be complicated. But she felt very comfortable with Sieg. She recognized that that comfort was one of the pitfalls of getting close to an attractive alcoholic.

Elizabeth answered the letters she received from both Graham Brown and David Nelson. That was one thing about life in Riyadh for a single Western woman, there was plenty of spare time for letter writing, and plenty of spare men. Gradually, David's letters dropped off in frequency as he became ensnared in the exciting life of the US capital. Graham's letters were regular with some Los Angeles news and several paragraphs of salacious references to what he would like to do the next time he saw her.

Elizabeth confessed to herself that she missed sex, no matter how dangerous it was to have unmarried sex in this fundamentalist Islamic city. She wondered why Sieg made no move toward the bedroom when he picked her up and entertained her in his flat. He opened and closed doors for her without touching her. They did not go to the few restaurants in hotels where western couples were welcome, as *mutawahs* had been know to follow western couples away from such restaurants and stop them in their car to verify their relationship. Elizabeth had heard of one couple who were married to different people who had been caught. He was simply giving the woman an innocent ride to the shopping mall. The *mutawah* examined the man's *igama* and the woman's visa. The two couples had been deported despite both men having important consultant jobs. Their Saudi sponsors could not protect them from the *mutawahs* and the Committee for the Promotion of Virtue and the Prevention of Vice.

Besides, Sieg was a good cook who enjoyed hosting. They often went to his flat after an evening music performance or a covert movie in someone's villa. One day he took her to the camel market where he paid one of the men to milk one of the camels into a bowl. He offered Elizabeth a drink before he consumed the remaining milk himself.He never made any sexual overtures. She wondered if it was because he was still married though he had said he just supported his wife financially because she was too mentally disabled to earn a salary herself. Eventually, Elizabeth built up enough courage to ask him if he was not attracted to her.

"My dear, I find you very attractive, but I have been impotent for many years, ever since before my last binge and dry-out," he explained.

"Have you given up on trying?" she questioned, feeling keenly the lack of affection from a sexual relationship.

"I guess I thought Saudi Arabia was a safe place to be for me to prevent me from drinking and from displaying my impotence," he said. "I have thought of trying again with the right person," he said, looking meaningfully at her, "but I have been scared I'd fail again which would make me believe even more that it's impossible for me to ever get an erection."

"Do you want to try?" she asked forthrightly.

"Yes, but I'm not ready to try tonight. I want everything to be just right, to be relaxed, clean sheets, soft music, everything. Can we try it that way soon?" he asked.

How could she refuse such a request?

Chapter 39

Sick Jamal

Amina's next letter showed that she had indeed discovered Jamal's exact diagnosis.   She still addressed her teacher formally.

Dear Mrs. Elizabeth,   *March 14, 1983*

Jamal's doctor told me diagnosis, human immunodeficiency virus. I am sure you know this new disease. Jamal was moved from Adventist Hospital to Los Angeles County Hospital where they will open a ward especially for human immunodeficiency virus patients. This hospital is closer so I able to visit him more often. They made me take human immunodeficiency virus test even though I told them we not ever have coitus. They no believe me until I took test.

Doctor says Jamal will have short life. If he die, some man my family have to bring me home. I want finish degree before he die so if family make me come back Riyadh, I can get teaching job University.

But I really want stay America. Family never agree! I worry. If Jamal die, Muslim man must be buried next day. There is mosque here but I no go. Very worry!

You come soon, summer holiday, yes?

Amina

It was indeed time for Elizabeth to prepare for the yearly home holiday. She could tell from Amina's writing that she was under great stress. Amina's English language had become much better than her classmates at National Saudia Women's University nursing program. But in this letter, she frequently left out prepositions and articles.

Was there anything she could do for Amina besides hold her hand and comfort her? She wondered if Amina's family knew Jamal was sick. Should she contact them and simply say she was going to see Amina soon. Did they have anything to send to her? Contacting them could be too risky as they might suspect something was up. She certainly should not do it without consulting Amina first.

So she calculated the time halfway around the world looking at the globe in the National Saudia Women's University library to see how many time zones different they were away. She had done this before coming to Saudi Arabia but she had forgotten. When it was seven in the evening in California, it was three in the morning in Saudi Arabia. She wanted to be sure that Amina would be in her apartment, perhaps studying. Being a regular sleeper, Elizabeth seldom set her alarm clock but on this occasion she made an exception. She was fearful of the alarm ringing loudly enough to awaken Ina in the other end of the flat so she put it under a pillow near her regular sleeping pillow to muffle it. She could never predict what might get a complaint from Ina. In fact sharing space with Ina was one of the most stressful parts of living in Riyadh for Elizabeth.

Sleepily she dialed the number trying to remember that the phone could be tapped and to use neutral words. "Amina, this is Elizabeth Adams in Riyadh."

"Oh, Mrs. Elizabeth, good to hear your voice!" Amina seemed on the edge of tears but it was hard to be sure over this distance as there were some echoes on the line.

"Amina, I am wondering if you want me to contact your family before I start my holiday and ask if they have anything they want to send to you." Elizabeth stated.

Amina did burst into tears so Elizabeth waited until she controlled herself enough to reply, "Hear your voice make me cry."

"You are under a great deal of stress, with your school work and visiting Jamal in the hospital. I will be there soon, so hold on. Shall I say anything to your family? Is there anything you want me to bring you like Arabic coffee or spices?" Elizabeth wanted to offer comfort which was hard at this distance.

"Yes, please, call my mother. I tell her things I want. She send driver with package to you to bring," Amina replied still tearful. "How much room you have in suitcase?"

The day before Sieg was to take Elizabeth to the airport, the little 'watch dog' in the university hospital flats knocked on her door and handed her a 12 inch by 12 inch by 5 inches bundle wrapped in the Arabic edition of *Al Arabia* newspaper and tied with twine. There was a tag with Arabic writing on it. Her own name in Arabic was one of the words she had learned to recognize as well as the number #404 for her flat. Even through the paper, Elizabeth could smell coriander. She knew it would make her suitcase smell really good by the time she got to Los Angeles. Would the customs agents think coriander was some sort of drug? They must be used to recognizing what was admissible and what was forbidden, she assumed. But she still felt a little anxiety about the package.

This was her fourth trip from Riyadh to Los Angeles. She felt like an old hand at this trip though this one would take her through Paris and Newark, New Jersey instead of her usual Atlanta route. She planned to stay three nights in Paris since she had never seen the city before. Because of the restriction about the two months bond in order to get a permission paper to leave the Kingdom, she had opted to take her other holidays like *hajj* in the Kingdom, traveling with Jessie and Amy to Dhahran and Jubbah to see more petroglyphs. Desert Rambler trips supplanted other international travel.

Graham Brown met her airplane in Los Angles. However, he delivered Elizabeth to her sister's home as he had become involved with another of his teaching colleagues and he did not feel free to invite Elizabeth to stay overnight as Graham and his new love had apparently become so comfortable that she had a key to his apartment and came and went sometimes without warning. Elizabeth knew this kind of relationship could happen with Graham while she was on the other side of the world for nine months a year. He had even hinted at it in his ever more infrequent letters.

Before he delivered her to her sister's house, he took her to Poor Richard's Restaurant on Slauson to share some hometown food.

"I hope I'll have a chance to introduce you to Carol while you are here. I think you would like her," Graham told Elizabeth as he carried her suitcase to her sister's door.

Ah well, Elizabeth told herself, in this day when

relationships came and went and changed, it was a situation to be accepted unless one wanted to give up an exciting overseas career.

The next morning, after making sure her own car would start running since her sister sometimes forgot to drive it often enough to keep the battery well charged, Elizabeth drove to West Los Angeles and picked up Amina. They went together to Los Angeles County General Hospital to visit Jamal. The AIDS patients were scattered through the hospital as they had not yet designated a special AIDS ward. They walked to the old towers, the nineteen story building visible from the freeway and entered the door under the statue of the Angel of Mercy. This hospital built in the 1930s was equal in decoration to Royal King Faisel Hospital in Riyadh but these murals portrayed real or mythical people and gods. No human images could be displayed in King Faisel Hospital except in medical charts and in books in the medical library.

Jamal was in the pulmonary ward in an isolation room with contagion precautions. As they walked, Amina said, "Jamal already mental. Make no sense when he talk. Slow to recognize me."

They had eventually gone though the door of the tiny room between the hallway and his room where they donned the contagion prevention booties, gloves, gowns and masks. They could see through the glass window, Jamal lying in a bed which looked like an adult version of a child's crib with sides which could be raised and lowered. It was unusual to allow two visitors at a time in these isolation rooms but Amina was known to the nurses due to her frequent visits and she was also persuasive about the need for Elizabeth to be allowed to go with her to see her husband.

He did not awaken when they closed the dressing room door behind them. They went and stood on either side of his crib bed. Amina said his name but did not reach out her gloved hand to touch him. His name was muffled coming through her face mask. She continued to say his name followed by some Arabic phrase which Elizabeth could not immediately translate despite having studied the language for several years. Eventually his eyes fluttered open.

"Mrs. Elizabeth, my teacher from Riyadh came to visit," Amina explained.

Jamal's eyes struggled to focus. Eventually he seemed to be able to fix her in his vision and he raised his hand from the blanket and then let it fall back. Suddenly, his body gave a shudder like a convulsion but less intense. His eyes rolled back momentarily. It was obvious that he was very, very sick.

After ten minutes with Amina talking in Arabic to Jamal and translating what she was saying for Elizabeth, and Jamal lying in his crib responding only with his eyes which followed Amina, the two women decided to leave. Before going, Amina lifted the plastic covered water glass and straw and tried to help Jamal drink but he batted it away. Amina set it on the small chest beside the bed. "Let us go," she said.

Chapter 35

The Mosque

"Will you take me to the mosque?" asked Amina as they drove out of the LA County General Hospital parking lot unto Marengo Street. She had been using taxis ever since Jamal entered the hospital since she was still not comfortable sitting on the public bus where any man could sit down beside her.

"Well, sure. When would you like to go? And where is the mosque here. Since women aren't allowed to pray in the Riyadh mosques, I've never been in one," Elizabeth replied.

"The mosque I know about is on Vermont Avenue downtown. Maybe we could go to Friday prayers after I finish my clinical," Amina suggested.

"Why do you want to go there?" questioned Elizabeth.

"Jamal die soon, doctor says. Then I have no *sohbah* here. Family will want me come home. I want finish degree. I no want tell them Jamal die till finish degree. I want bury him here so need to talk to *Imam* about what required," Amina explained.

"Won't his family be worried? Don't they talk with him

or write to him?" she questioned.

"When they call, I say he in class. They no know he in hospital." She did not glance at Elizabeth who was looking sideways at her while driving.

Elizabeth considered how Amina's language was still not smooth. She wondered how she was communicating with her American patients and the faculty. Elizabeth decided she needed to spend more time with Amina working on her English language skills. But right now, she wondered what to respond to Amina.

Elizabeth agreed to pick Amina up from her graduate clinical in Cedar Sinai Hospital in West Hollywood before evening prayers on Friday.

Meanwhile, Elizabeth was able to connect with some of her former nursing colleagues who updated her on news and gossip. She mentioned nothing of the Amina/Jamal dilemma to them. And there was always shopping to do for things unavailable in Saudi Arabia, such as certain vitamins and make-up for her lighter colored skin.

Friday, she picked up Amina and they drove to the mosque. Amina led her to the small section off in the back corner of the main room with a two and one half foot wooden accordion fence which confined the women. The men assembled in the larger open space of what had formerly been a bank. They all sat on the floor. There were women with babies which they lay on the carpet covered floor beside where they sat. Gradually, the space filled up so the women's section was quite crowded. The women, including Elizabeth and Amina, all had head scarves, *hijabs*, but none had their faces covered. The men's section also filled with men milling about as the *imam* ascended the *minbar*, the pulpit. He was dressed in California 'casual' with navy slacks and a short sleeved blue chambray shirt and a small white cotton crotched cap on the back of his head. He began his sermon in Arabic language and Elizabeth recognized only a few words such as *Allah*. The *imam* spoke for nearly half an hour. One young mother rose and took her crying baby outside. The *adhan*, prayer call, was called out by the *muezzin*. All the men and women rolled out their prayer rugs and started the rituals of Islamic prayer. Elizabeth slid further into the back corner hoping it was not obvious that she was not praying. The other women behind the little wooden fence seemed totally absorbed in their prayers, apparently completely ignoring anyone but *Allah*, the one God.

Elizabeth thought how ironic it was that she had spent several years in Saudi Arabia and yet this was the first time she had visited a mosque or been this close to praying Muslims. But women were not allowed in mosques in Riyadh as she learned from what her students told her.

Amina waited until almost all the men and women had departed before walking around the edge of the floor where the men's prayer rugs were still lined up on the floor and knocked on the door with the sign *Imam* in English and Arabic إمام.

"*Udkhul*," Enter, said the voice. Amina realized his Arabic language had an Egyptian accent but Elizabeth was still new enough to the Arabic language that she did not recognize the different accents unless it was pointed out to her specifically which Amina was too distressed to do.

Amina timidly pushed the door open, stood just inside

and introduced herself and Elizabeth in English while keeping her eyes downcast. Saudi women seldom spoke to *imams* as they were not *maharram* - a safe male for a woman to be with. She still wore her nurse's uniform with her head scarf.

Immediately the *imam* changed to English. "What can I do for you, my sisters?"

Amina hesitated as she would have preferred to speak her native Arabic but she knew Elizabeth needed to understand it as well so, "My husband will die soon the doctor say. I want to be able to follow Saudi Arabian custom bury him immediately. You know in Saudi Arabia, women no attend funerals. What should I do here?"

"Where is your husband? What is his affliction?" The *imam* asked.

"He in Los Angeles County Hospital. He has human immunodeficiency virus," she said quickly hoping that the *imam* did not know the complete medical name of AIDS and would simply take what she said as any other fatal disease.

However, an *imam* in a big sophisticated city like Los Angeles could not be ignorant of this plague and he knew also that some of the young men in his congregation who had died recently were all surreptitious homosexuals who had died of the named disease. The Health Department made sure that all AIDS burials were done in a way to avoid communicating the disease as it was still unknown the exact route of transmission. Like clergy in ever religion, they were not easily shocked. But he did not want to drive

Amina off from the services of this center of Los Angeles' Muslim community so he replied, "My daughter, does he have other family here?"

"No," she responded, "I am his only family here. He was a student at Occidental College until he was too sick. His family is all in Riyadh. Cannot come here!" She spoke emphatically but still avoiding the gaze of the *imam*.

"When your husband dies, contact me," he said handing her a paper with his telephone number at his office in the mosque and in his home. He was a family man and did much of his study for his sermons in his den at home in nearby Glendale in a predominantly Arab neighborhood. He did not offer to go and visit Jamal as he did not particularly like hospitals or associating with homosexuals. Actually, he wanted the two women to leave as soon as possible as some of the men who had died recently, he knew had been bisexual and this *imam* wondered if Amina also carried the disease. He did not want them in his office any longer.

Amina said, "In Saudi Arabia, women not go to the graveyard to bury men. Who will bury him here? Where will he be buried? I will pay for what is needed."

The *imam*, eager to have this conversation over, replied, "Call me when he dies, I will take care of everything. You can donate money to the mosque afterward." He arose from his desk indicating the session was over.

As they drove away in the car hot from the late June afternoon sun, Amina gave way to tears, tears she had not shed since Elizabeth had first met with her after she arrived in Los Angles. She wiped her eyes with her *hijab*, her head scarf.

Elizabeth got the air conditioning going so the car cooled as they drove back to Amina's apartment. Though it was still light outside, the night life of a Friday in Los Angles was just warming up with people entering restaurants, theaters and bars.

Two days before Elizabeth was to depart for Riyadh, Amina called to say that, "Jamal died. Imam need me to sign papers. Jamal already buried by Health Department. Can you drive me to imam's office? Imam take care of everything."

"Have you told your family and his family that Jamal died?" asked Elizabeth when she picked Amina up.

"No, I am not going to tell them. I want to finish degree. If my family know I am here alone, my brother or father come get me. If they call, I tell lies. I say Jamal busy," Amina explained.

Chapter 36

Epilogue

Upon her return to the University Hospital flats, Elizabeth found #404 empty. She learned from Jessie that her roommate Ina, had been arrested for making *Sediki*, the slang name for homemade liquor in her room at the back of the flat. That, Elizabeth realized, was why she was always so private and kept her bedroom door locked. Ina had maintained distance between herself and the other faculty. She had developed her business in the more lenient King Faisal years before any other Westerners were hired for the Nursing Department. One of her clients, apparently, felt she cheated him on the price and turned her in to the Committee for the Promotion of Virtue and the Prevention of Vice. She had been arrested and deported back to the USA within twenty-four hours. They had confiscated all the distilling equipment and unsold bottles. Some had been broken in the raid and the smell lingered in the felt floor cover. There were also lingering slivers of glass.

First, Elizabeth vacuumed up the slivers of glass, then took an inventory of the flat. Ina had left most of her possessions and certainly all her furniture, though they had allowed her to come back and pack a suitcase before she was driven to her flight. Elizabeth decided to occupy Ina's bedroom, in the 'women's section' and let the new faculty member whom they would hire to replace Ina, have Elizabeth's bedroom and bathroom in the 'men's section' near the front door. With the help of Jessie and Amy, she moved the remainder of Ina's possessions to the front bedroom. She moved her own things into the back. It took several weeks for the smell of alcohol to dissipate.

At the university, as soon as she had finished arranging her class schedule and syllabi, she began to work on the slide show for her presentation for the upcoming November Athens nursing education conference. She had to ask the Dean's office for slides of the buildings and campus because their pictures always made sure not to have any human figures in their photos. She planned to augment these slides with ones she had taken surreptitiously with her 35 millimeter Canon Sure Shot.

She had had a letter from Graham Brown telling that he had broken up with Carol, the teacher he had been dating last summer, the one that made it so Elizabeth could not spend time with him. Apparently, Carol had been too 'clingy' something he could not tolerate which was why he was still single at forty, he explained. He planned to take some extra time for his Thanksgiving vacation and meet her in Athens as they had planned before he and Carol became intimate. He hoped she was not angry about not being together last summer.

Elizabeth was pleased as she missed that kind of intimacy. She quickly wrote a letter agreeing with his plan. She mailed it to him at the main post office.

Ever since the October 23, 1983 US Marine Barracks bombing in Beirut, there had been a little bit more tension for Americans flying in the Middle East. However, after three years in Riyadh, Elizabeth had grown a little "*Que sera, sera*" French for 'what ever will be will be' about the dangers of travel. Perhaps Elizabeth had been in Saudi Arabia so long she had absorbed their *En Sha Allah*, If God Wills It, attitude. There had been bombing threats at the Riyadh Consulate so that metal detectors had been installed. All forms of travel had been more threatened by apparently powerless men who used the techniques of abduction and threats of violence to achieve some sort of power for themselves.

Patsy Elgin had indeed been reprimanded by the California Board of Registered Nursing. However, a reprimand was not enough to keep her from being hired by a nursing school in Karachi, Pakistan. At this time, Pakistan was in its usual political turmoil in relation to the United States, so consequently Patsy avoided having The Pakistan Nursing Council and her Pakistani University nursing school administration discover her reprimand. Their desperation to have English speakers teaching their nursing classes had compelled them to hire her anyway. That university was generous with allowing faculty to attend conferences. Thus she was able to hear Elizabeth's presentation in Athens and slip out before being confronted face-to-face. When Elizabeth learned after the presentation by inquiring of the conference organizers from where Patsy Elgin had sent her conference registration, she took the address and began a campaign of letter writing to Patsy. When her letters were ignored, Elizabeth enlisted Jessie Edwards, Director of the National Saudia University for Girls Nursing Program to write a letter to the director of the Karachi nursing program describing Patsy's theft from both Aisha and Elizabeth. Patsy's teaching contract was not renewed. Her crime was only documented in the California Board of Registered Nursing files, not in the criminal justice system. Nonetheless, she became a pariah as her reputation spread and she was unable to get another teaching job in any credible nursing school. But nurses were in so much demand in the United States since nursing educations programs were perennially short of qualified faculty that student enrollment was limited. Consequently, there were never enough nurses. Patsy was finally able to get a regular nursing job at the Louisiana State Penitentiary in Angola. Working in the infirmary of a prison is stressful due to the dangerous natures of prisoners. Nurses must always be on alert even when accompanied by a prison guard. Despite the ever-present guard, she was still occasionally attacked while taking blood pressures or temperatures of patients in shackles. She spent her career in the company of other thieves and also murderers. When Elizabeth learned via the nursing grapevine of Patsy's situation, she felt she had gotten her just desserts even though her debt was still outstanding.

Amina Khoury took four more years to finish her master's degree at UCLA. During those years, she wrote letters to both hers and Jamal's families as if he were still alive, lying about his health, activities and their desire to stay in the USA until they both finished their degrees. When Occidental University notified the Saudi government that Jamal was no longer enrolled, they simply stopped his tuition and living expense payments but because his last name Badawy, was different from Amina's, her payments continued. There were too many Saudi students studying in the USA for the Saudi funding office to investigate the situation.

Amina did not want to go back to Riyadh after five years

in the USA enjoying the freedoms allowed women there. She finally told both families that Jamal had died and that she was a widow. When her family demanded her return, she applied for US refugee status which was granted and she eventually attained US residency and eventually citizenship. Nurses were in high demand in all US hospitals and clinics, but particularly nurses with special skills such as Amina's. She took a job in an Egyptian doctor's private practice in the Arab neighborhood in Glendale. Her master's level skills far surpassed the requirements of a doctor's office nurse, but it allowed her to get her green card until she got her citizenship. Her family continued to try to get her to come home to Riyadh. Often when other Saudis visited Los Angeles they sought her out to present her family's pleas to return to Riyadh. But she had enjoyed her freedoms and was unwilling to put herself under the protection of a male guardian which is what would have been required, had she returned. Even a visit from her sister and Fatimah with husband and by now three children could not persuade her.

Eventually, as happened with almost all expatriate Americans in Saudi Arabia, Sieg Meyer decided to retire back in the US. After years of working in the US Treasury he was assured of a generous government pension. His time in Riyadh as a consultant to the Ministry of Finance had also been lucrative as he had had to pay no taxes on that salary. This had not solved his impotence problem, though. He and Elizabeth had tried more than once to get him aroused enough for an erection. While they had both enjoyed the effort, success evaded them. He had returned to Washington D.C. They remained friends with letters, phone calls and visits cross-country after Elizabeth returned to the USA until Sieg succumbed to a heart attack at age seventy-five. She felt lucky it had never happened during their time in Riyadh together. What if he had had a heart attack during one of their efforts to achieve an erection? She might have indeed been arrested by the Committee for the Promotion of Virtue and the Prevention of Vice. In her imagination, she fantasized herself getting dressed and calling the ambulance just before fleeing the scene.

In time, Elizabeth Adams decided it was time to get her doctorate if she planned to stay in the university teaching system. After applying to a number of doctoral degree programs, she was accepted into another nearby University of California special cultural studies doctoral program which was impressed with her Saudi Arabia teaching experiences. She took this offer of acceptance into a public university doctoral program rather than some more famous private university program because she would be able to pay 'in-state' tuition as she had maintained her California address during all her years in Riyadh. She utilized her slowly acquired Arabic language skills and her continuing friendship with Amina to design a research protocol examining responses of various nationalities of Arabs in the American healthcare system.

The End

Glossary

Abaya – black floor length cloak for women

Adhan – first call to prayer

Ahlan wa Sahlan – You are one of us and are welcome.

Akhu – brother

Allah – the one God

Amina – faithful

Amm – uncle

Baba-ganoush – roasted eggplant dip

Bedu –shortening of the word Bedouin

Dallah - the Arabic coffee pot

En Sha Allah – If God wills it

Fairuz – turquoise

Flooze – money

Galabaya - caftan

Ghutra – head-scarf worn by Arab men

Hajj – Muslim pilgrimage to Mecca

Hijab – scarf to cover hair

Hookah – water pipe for tobacco

Hummus – ground chickpeas

Igama – foreign worker's visa

Igal – black rings men place on top of their ghutra,

Jebel - a rock ridge

Jihad – striving against enemies of Islam

Jinn – supernatural creatures

Khatab - matchmaker

Kole – eye shadow, thought to originate in Egypt

Ma Salama – Be Safe! Or colloquially for Goodbye

Maharram - a safe male for a woman to be with; father, brother, son or husband

Minbar – pulpit from which imam gives sermons

Mouna – desire or wish

Muezzin – man who makes the call to prayer

Mustashfaa – hospital

Mutawahs –religious police

Niqab – The veil that leaves just a slit for the eyes

Nour – light

Riyal – Saudi money designation worth about 33¢ in 1980

Shia - branch of Islam with many believers in Iran, Syria

& Turkey

Sohbah –safe company

Souq – market place

Sunni – the largest of Islam's denomination based on the Sunnah, customs from verbally

transmitted teachings

Surah – division in the *Koran* like chapter in the *Bible*.

Thobe – white gown worn by Arab men

Shawarma – a Mediterranean sandwich

Ude- musical instrument something like a mandolin

Udkhul – Enter

Ululate – vocalization by fast tongue movement

Wadi – a dry river except in rainy season

Wudu – ritual ablutions

Reference List

A Season in Mecca: Narrative of A Pilgrimage (2005) Abdellah Hammoudi, Farrar & Strauss. NY.

A US Feminist in Saudi Arabia: 1980-1982 (1983 & 2010) Margaret Drake, iUniverse, Bloomington, Indiana.

At the Drop of a Veil (1971) Marianne Aliresa, Houghton Mifflin, NY.

Confessions of an Innocent Man: Torture and Survival in a Saudi Prison (2005) William Sampson, McClelland & Stewart Ltd, Toronto, Ontario.

Ghost Wars: The Secret History of the CIA, Afghanistan, and Bin Laden, from Soviet Invasion to September 10, 2001, (2004) Steve Coll, Penguin Books, NY.

Guests of the Sheik (1969) Elizabeth Warnock Fernea, Doubleday Anchor, NY.

If The Oceans Were Ink: An Unlikely Friendship and a Journey to the Heart of the Quran (2015) Carla Power, Henry Holt Company, NY.

Jihad in Islamic History: Doctrines and Practice (2006) Michael Bonner, Princeton, NJ.

Middle Eastern Muslim Women Speak (1977) edited by Elizabeth Warnock Fernea and Basima Qattan Bezirgan, University of Texas Press, Austin.

Sandstorms: Days and Nights in Arabia (1991) Peter

Theroux, W.W. Norton & Co., NY.

The Doomed Oasis, (1960) Hammond Innes, Alfred A. Knopf, NY.

The Glorious Kur`an: Translation and Commentary (1931) Abdallah Yousef Ali

When the Moon is Low (2015) Nadia Hashimi, Morrow, NY.

Women in the Muslim World (1978) Lois Beck and Nikki Keddie, Harvard Univeristy Press, Cambridge, MA.

Sukoon Magazine http://www.sukoonmag.com/responsive/

MAP OF THE REGION

Cast of Characters

(In Order of Appearance)

Elizabeth Adams RN – main character

Aunt Sephrena – Aunt of Elizabeth Adams

Aunt Phyllis – Aunt of Elizabeth Adams

Mrs. Planchette –Elizabeth's influential high school teacher

Patsy Elgin – nurse who left the others with her debt

Jessie Edwards RN – Director of the Nursing Education Program at National Saudi

University for Girls

Jenna – Jessie's daughter

Graham Brown – US lover, HS math teacher

Carol –Graham's new girlfriend in 1983

Dean Ashwari - Dean of Health Sciences School at National Saudi University for Girls

Aisha Al Aben – Egyptian nursing faculty member at National Saudi University for Girls

Ina Brook – First roommate and faculty member at National Saudi University for Girls

Mr. Rahman – The Dean's aide, National Saudi University for Girls Health Sciences

School

Amal – Nursing School secretary, National Saudi University for Girls

Amy Burch – Teacher of psychiatry, National Saudi University for Girls Nursing

Program

Chuck Toiler –Jessie & Amy's friend from Riyadh International Christian   Fellowship

Rev. Davis – Minister at Riyadh International Christian Fellowship

Mildred Davis - The minister's wife

Samia – Amy's Egyptian office mate

Nour – Elizabeth's Egyptian office mate who taught the first lab with wound care, bed

    bathes, etc.

Dr. and Mrs. Clough – Australian employee of WHO

David Nelson – American Army consultant

Claire – David's almost ex-wife

Amina Khoury– First name means Faithful, a student

Aunt Maymunah – Amina's aunt

Fairuz Maloof – Turquoise, a student, family of doctors.

Mouna Shamoon – First name means Desire or wish, the student who came late the first

day. She has a Syrian mother, and has brown hair.

Ferdooz – the one senior nursing student

Nouri – Nursing department tea lady

Mr. Amari– University driver from Yemen

Head Nurse Najjar – med-surg head nurse at Shemazzi

Dr. Awad – Shemazzi Hospital Medical Director

Fareeda Seddik – the Shemazzi surgical nurse who takes the students on ward tour

Mahmoud – Fairuz's pulmonologist intern brother.

Dr. Deng, dark skinned Sudanese surgeon, head of med/surg at Shemazzi

Dr. Fadel – who flirts with Elizabeth during rounds at Shemazzi.

Kenneth – winemaker

Jenny McFarlane- Scottish nurse, at the National Guard Hospital

Abdul – Amina's prospective brother-in-law

Mrs. Sohair - Egyptian faculty colleague

Hamza - the Saudi National Guard officer who consults with David

General Badawy – father of Jamal and has six sons

Jamal Badawy – homosexual in National Guard

Ali Badawy- his next older brother of the six Badawy boys

Imad – Bahraini lover of Jamal

Dr. Christine Ribon - Director of the Masters in Nursing Program UCLA

Siegfried Meyer – Treasury Ministry consultant

www.ingramcontent.com/pod-product-compliance
Lightning Source LLC
Chambersburg PA
CBHW071233210726
48293CB00002B/683